A prince was kissing her?

Was she dreaming? Perhaps she was still standing at the sink, her hands in soapy water while she watched his press conference and fantasized about him. But she was no Cinderella.

And this was no dream.

His lips were warm and real and surprisingly silky given the hard look of his mouth and the firmness of his jaw. He deepened the kiss, and she willingly followed where he led her. She kissed him back.

She had never known such tenderness and couldn't believe that a man who'd fought as hard as he had to protect her was capable of it. Maybe it was gratitude over his saving her that drew her to him.

He said he wouldn't hurt her and she wanted to believe him. But mostly she just wanted him.

But why would Sebastian want her? He was a prince. They had no future together even if someone wasn't determined to kill her.

LISA CHILDS

RANSOM FOR A PRINCE

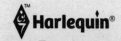

TORONTO NEW YORK LONDON
AMSTERDAM PARIS SYDNEY HAMBURG
STOCKHOLM ATHENS TOKYO MILAN MADRID
PRAGUE WARSAW BUDAPEST AUCKLAND

With special thanks to Melissa Jeglinski for being
a fabulous agent and a wonderful friend.

Special thanks and acknowledgment to Lisa Childs
for her contribution to the Cowboys Royale series.

ISBN-13: 978-0-373-69530-0

RANSOM FOR A PRINCE

Recycling programs
for this product may
not exist in your area.

www.eHarlequin.com

Printed in U.S.A.

ABOUT THE AUTHOR

Bestselling, award-winning author Lisa Childs writes paranormal and contemporary romance for Harlequin Books. She lives on thirty acres in west Michigan with her husband, two daughters, a talkative Siamese and a long-haired Chihuahua who thinks she's a Rottweiler. Lisa loves hearing from readers, who can contact her through her website, www.lisachilds.com, or snail mail address, P.O. Box 139, Marne, MI 49435.

Books by Lisa Childs

HARLEQUIN INTRIGUE
 664—RETURN OF THE LAWMAN
 720—SARAH'S SECRETS
 758—BRIDAL RECONNAISSANCE
 834—THE SUBSTITUTE SISTER
1213—MYSTERY LOVER
1263—RANSOM FOR A PRINCE

CAST OF CHARACTERS

Prince Sebastian Cavanaugh—Desperate for information on his missing friend, this ruler and former military marksman offers a reward to bring the witness to him. He never imagines that the reward she'll claim will be his heart and maybe his life.

Jessica Peters—The single mother has kept quiet about what she witnessed in order to protect herself and others. But when Prince Sebastian draws her out, he also draws out feelings she'd never thought she'd feel again and danger they might not survive.

Samantha Peters—The four-year-old has never known her father, but she wants to get to know the prince and find out if fairy tales can come true.

Helen Jeffries—The ranch owner needs money; but does she need it desperately enough to betray her friend?

Prince Antoine Cavanaugh—Co-ruler with his twin brother, Sebastian, of the island nation of Barajas, the former military interrogator will do *whatever* necessary to protect his brother.

Brenner—The chief of security for the corulers of Barajas may prove himself unworthy of their trust.

Dmitri—A hired gun who knows his mission in Wind River, Wyoming, will not end well for anyone.

Danny Harold—The reporter knows too much and perhaps reveals too much, as well.

Evgeny Surinka—All the man wants is his wife. And revenge…

Chapter One

"Mama, is he a real prince? Like in my stories, like the one who kissed Sleeping Beauty?"

Jessica glanced up from the sink of dishes to focus on the television on the counter nearest the farmhouse table. She had turned the channel to cartoons for Samantha to watch while the four-year-old ate her breakfast, but the screen displayed no animated figures. Just a tall man in a dark, tailored suit.

As a reporter announced that Prince Sebastian Cavanaugh had called this press conference at the sheriff's office, a camera zoomed in on the royal's face. It was all chiseled features—rigid jaw, aristocratic cheekbones beneath intense, dark blue eyes and his nose was just slightly bent in an arrogant tilt. She doubted it could have once been broken. After all, he was a prince—privileged and protected.

He was one of the five rulers of island nations in the Mediterranean, who had, along with their entourages, converged on Dumont, Wyoming, for a summit meeting two weeks ago. That meeting had yet to occur.

Jessica didn't need to listen to the press conference to learn why; she already knew. Too well. Every time she closed her eyes she saw *why:* the flames illuminating the night sky, rising up from the charred metal of the limousine she'd been following from the Wind River Ranch and Resort. If only the fire was all she'd seen...

Her breath hitching, she blinked open her eyes and focused on the television again. And on the prince. She lost herself in the depths of those dark blue eyes as he stepped up to the mic at the podium set up in the sheriff's office, which was located in the Wind River County Courthouse.

"Mama?" Samantha asked, her voice soft with confusion.

Jessica never ignored her daughter, but she still couldn't tear her gaze from the screen.

"I am Prince Sebastian Cavanaugh, coruler with my brother, Antoine, of the island nation of Barajas."

The little girl's breath shuddered out with a gasp of awe. "He is a real prince."

"Yes," Jessica murmured—finally—in acknowledgment.

"Barajas," Cavanaugh continued, "is part of COIN, the Coalition of Island Nations consisting of Kyros, Nadar and Jamala, that came to your country—and your particular county—for a special summit to discuss trade agreements that would benefit the United States as well as COIN."

Cameras flashed in his face as reporters interrupted with questions. A burly man, perhaps one of the royal's security detail, stepped closer to the prince and leaned toward the microphone as if to warn the media to back off. But Prince Sebastian turned to him, an intense look in his eyes, and the man shrank back. Then the prince turned that stare on the reporters and the questions stopped, an eerie silence descending on the crowded outer office.

"Since our arrival, we have been under attack." A muscle twitched in his lean cheek just above the tightly clenched jaw. "There have been vocal protests of our visit to your country. And there have been physical protests. On our first night here, an explosion occurred which killed a man."

Jessica flinched but kept her eyes open so that she wouldn't see again that horror. But it didn't matter. The image was forever burned in her mind, like the body had burned.

"We have recently been made aware that there was a witness to that explosion," Prince Cavanaugh continued. "We need this witness to come forward as we believe he or she has vital information."

Jessica gasped. How had they found out? Who else might know that she'd been traveling that same road and had come upon the scene? She shivered.

The camera zoomed in on the prince. While an aura of arrogance and authority clung to the man's broad shoulders and rigidly clenched jaw, he buried that pride as his gaze implored the witness to share what she knew. "This is a matter of life and death. A friend of mine—" his voice was gruff with emotion "—has been missing since the explosion. I am offering a substantial reward for information that will lead to his return."

After another beat of silence from the reporters, the room erupted with questions. They shouted over each other, so their voices were unintelligible.

Prince Sebastian fixed that stare on the crowd again until they subsided to just excited murmurs. "One question at a time," he directed them.

"How much is the reward?" Danny Harold asked. The reporter from the local television station had pushed closest to the podium.

The prince's reply had the crowd gasping with surprise and awe.

"So it's Sheik Amir Khalid who is missing?" Danny tossed out another question. "Do you believe he's still alive or do you suspect he's dead?"

The intensity of Prince Cavanaugh's gaze changed from intimidation and arrogance to anguish and frustration. "We do not have enough information to determine the sheik's whereabouts or his physical condition."

"And you believe this witness might know where he or his body is?" Although many other reporters crowded the room, it was Danny who asked this question, too. Maybe it was because he was a local that his interest in the story seemed so personal.

The muscle twitched again in the prince's lean cheek.

"That is what we believe and why we are offering such a substantial reward."

Danny snorted. "That substantial reward is going to have every kook coming out of the woodwork with a cockamamie story so they can claim the money."

"Kooks?" the prince repeated, arching a golden brown brow.

"Crazies, crackpots," Danny translated.

Prince Sebastian's lips—the bottom one full and sensual—curved into a slight grin. "My brother, Prince Antoine, has a way of determining when a person is telling the truth or a lie."

Danny nodded in agreement. "He was an interrogator with military special forces."

The prince neither confirmed nor denied the reporter's statement. He just stared again, his blue eyes unblinking.

"And you were a sniper."

"Any more *questions?*" Prince Cavanaugh asked.

Jessica had many. So did her daughter.

"What's a matter, Mama?" The little girl slid out of her chair to join Jessica at the sink. She tugged on her soapy hand to gain her mother's attention.

"Nothing," Jessica replied as she turned toward her daughter. The sun streaming through the windows glinted off the little girl's honey brown hair and sparkled in her gray eyes, highlighting the child's concern. Jessica forced a reassuring smile. "I just got caught up in the news, like you sometimes do your cartoons."

"Didn't you ever seen a prince before?"

Jessica wasn't exactly certain what she'd seen that night except that it was probably enough to put her daughter and her in danger. Well, more danger than they were already in.

"There're no such things as princes," a husky but feminine voice murmured as Helen Jeffries joined them in the kitchen. The tall woman stomped her boots on the woven rug at the back door, knocking off mud and straw.

"Is, too," Samantha said, pointing at the television screen. "He's a real prince."

Helen snorted. "He might legally be a prince, but I've yet to meet a man who's a *real* prince."

The little girl's forehead scrunched up with confusion. "The ones in my books and movies aren't real?"

"Fairy tales," Helen replied cynically. "Not real."

"What about Clay McGuire?" Jessica asked about the rancher Helen dated.

The older woman snorted again. "He's a cowboy."

"Can't princes be cowboys?" Samantha asked.

Jessica chucked her daughter's slightly pointed chin. "You got that backward, honey."

The little girl's forehead wrinkled with confusion. "How?"

"Cowboys can't be princes," Helen explained with a grin. She stepped closer to the sink and dipped her hands into the sudsy water.

"You should have let me feed the animals," Jessica said. Then she would have missed that special report.

Helen shook her head. She'd owned and managed the Double J alone for years. The older woman was so fiercely independent and proud that she insisted on doing more of the chores herself. Jessica was proud, too, though and had convinced Helen to accept her help in lieu of the room and board she refused to let Jessica pay her. "I'd rather work in the barn than the kitchen," Helen said as she brushed a fingertip across Samantha's button nose, leaving a dab of foam on the upturned tip of it.

Jessica lifted up her daughter and hugged her sweet-smelling body close. "Sweetheart, why don't you run up to your room and change out of your pajamas and into your clothes?"

"Do I have school today?" Samantha asked, her gray eyes bright with hope.

Preschool was in session today, but Jessica didn't dare bring Samantha into town when it was overrun with media. "No school. You have work to do here instead, young lady. You have to pick up all the toys in your room."

"There're not that many, Mama," Samantha said, wriggling down from her arms.

Jessica's heart clutched with sadness that it was true. She wasn't able to afford everything her little girl deserved. "You still have to pick them up."

Samantha, feet dragging, headed up the back stairwell

in the kitchen. The house was a foursquare, two-story farmhouse. It had a large foyer with a grand staircase as well as the back stairwell. It also had more bedrooms than they needed. Now. But the ranch owner had plans to someday turn her home into a women's shelter. She'd put her plan in motion when she'd offered Jessica shelter more than four years ago.

Helen narrowed her eyes and focused on Jessica. "What's going on? You never lie to her."

"I have," Jessica regretfully admitted. Every time the little girl asked about her father.

With understanding Helen nodded. "Why won't you bring her to school?"

"It's too dangerous."

"School is too dangerous?"

"It's too dangerous for us to go to town right now." The prince's press conference had whipped the media into a frenzy, and they'd already been doing too much filming around Wind River County and the town of Dumont.

If she'd been caught on camera…

Helen sighed. "Crazy stuff going on since those damn royals came to Dumont. That explosion. Gunfire. And poor Clay…" His family had been among the most vocal protestors of the COIN summit. Now his youngest boy sat in jail.

"Mr. McGuire will be okay," Jessica assured her friend. "He has you."

Helen shrugged as if she wasn't so worried that

Jessica usually found her staring at the TV into the early hours of the morning instead of sleeping. "He's busy. I'm busy. We just see each other occasionally, you know. Nothing serious."

Was that really because they were too busy or because they both had their reasons for avoiding involvement? Jessica understood their reasons; she had her own. But then the prince's face filled the television screen again as the station replayed the earlier live broadcast. His deep blue gaze implored the witness to come forward, to ease some of his anxiety over his missing friend.

"Can you watch Samantha for me for a little while?" she asked the older woman.

Helen nodded. "Of course I can. And I don't blame you. That's a lot of money."

"I'm not claiming the reward."

"But, Jess—"

"I need to pick up my last check from the Wind River Ranch and Resort." She'd worked part-time as a dishwasher there because she had thought she would be safe hiding away in the hotel kitchen. She'd been wrong. About everything. "Then I'm packing up Samantha's and my things and leaving the Double J."

Helen gasped in surprise.

"You probably thought that you'd never get rid of us—"

"Never wanted to, honey, you know that," her friend assured her. "I don't want you to go now."

"I have to," Jessica insisted. "It's getting too dangerous

here. I should have left earlier—right after it happened. Hell, I should have left before the royals even arrived. I knew their meeting would bring the media down on Dumont."

But she hadn't expected the rest of it: the explosion, the murder...

"PRINCE SEBASTIAN, I wish you wouldn't have done that," Sheriff Jake Wolf said with a long-suffering sigh.

The younger man had had his hands full since they'd come to his county for their summit meeting. According to what the royals had learned, Wolf had already had enough to deal with since getting elected the year before, like corruption within his department and perhaps within the police department of Dumont. That was why Sebastian had chosen the sheriff's office in which to announce the reward for information.

"You agreed to the press conference," he reminded him.

"The amount of the reward you offered is the problem." Wolf groaned. "Danny Harold was right. It'll draw out every kook. Hell, it already is drawing 'em out." He gestured toward his deputies and office staff, all of whom were on a phone.

"It's been a couple of weeks since the explosion, but this witness has yet to come forward," Sebastian pointed out, frustration gnawing at his tense stomach.

"Apparently this person needs more incentive than the satisfaction of doing the right thing."

"Or he or she is too scared to come forward," the sheriff replied.

With good cause, too, given the evidence that had recently come to light. The royals had only just learned about the witness when Sheik Efraim Aziz discovered a posting on a special internet bulletin board that had promised to "take care" of the witness.

"The proper incentive has been known to make a person overcome his deepest fears," Sebastian said. But how would the witness know he was in danger unless someone had acted upon the "hit" put out on him?

"Maybe this person isn't able to come forward anymore." The sheriff voiced Sebastian's deepest fear.

If the witness had already been disposed of, then he and his friends may never discover what had happened to Amir. They wouldn't know if he, too, had already been disposed of.

One of the deputies stood up and gestured wildly for the sheriff's attention. When Wolf headed toward the young man's desk, Sebastian followed, his pulse quickening in anticipation. "What is it?" the sheriff asked.

"The prince is actually right here," the deputy replied—but to the caller, not his superior. He pressed his palm over the receiver and held it out. "She'll speak to only you, Your Highness."

Despite the trepidation clutching his heart, Sebastian reached for the phone with a steady hand. He had learned long ago to control his physical reactions because he'd had to have a steady finger on the trigger. But he couldn't control the curse from slipping through his lips when he heard only a dial tone.

"She's gone?" the deputy asked.

Sebastian jerked his head in a rough nod. "Did you get the number from the caller ID?"

"It was blocked," the young man replied.

"Can you trace it?"

The deputy's face flushed. "I don't think the call lasted long enough."

"Then maybe she is coming here—to talk to me. Maybe she only wanted to know if I was here." That had to be it. To collect the money for her eyewitness account, or her cockamamy story if the persistent reporter and the sheriff were correct, she needed to talk to him.

"Or she's setting up a trap," Sheriff Wolf said. "You and the other royals have been threatened. There have been previous attempts on some of your lives."

Sebastian gave in to a slight grin. "You believe it is now my turn?"

"And thanks to that press conference you just held, they know where you are."

"So they will storm the courthouse to kill me?"

"Prince Stefan was nearly shot outside this very building, his security guard killed," the sheriff reminded him, his voice pitched low so that any of the lingering reporters would not overhear. "These are bold criminals."

The royals had been warned that they were all in danger even before they'd landed on American soil. Then the limo had exploded, probably when someone had suspected they would all be riding in it. No one had been able to determine who was behind the explosion, so they were still in danger. "We have taken precautions."

"Your security force?" the sheriff scoffed.

"It is true that some of our men have proven themselves without honor and allegiance."

"As you said, with the proper incentive…"

Money. Vengeance. Jealousy. Sebastian wasn't certain exactly what had compelled their men to turn against them, and because of that, he wasn't certain he could trust any of the others to not turn as well. "That is why I must remain here, in case the witness does want to talk to me. No one else can be trusted."

"No one?" the sheriff asked, his jaw tensing with anger.

"It is not only our security team that has been bribed."

"True." Law enforcement had also been involved in some of the attacks.

"Because no one can be trusted, we have no option but to protect ourselves."

The sheriff shook his head. "You have another option. Go home. Go back to your islands and away from the danger and let me do my job without your interference."

"We will not leave until our friend is found."

"Then I hope like hell that was the witness on the phone and that she's coming in to talk to you."

Sebastian narrowed his eyes and studied the younger man's face. Was he telling the truth? Of everyone Sebastian had met in Wyoming, he almost trusted Sheriff Wolf. But with lives at stake, he couldn't allow himself to trust anyone but Antoine. "I can take care of myself, Sheriff."

"Danny was right about your military training?"

Sebastian nodded.

"But being a sniper is different than being the one who's hunted. In the service, you remained a safe distance from the action. If you stay here, you can't."

"I'm not certain Barajas would be a safe distance from the action." There was a chance that his and his brother's enemies had been behind the explosion in hope of killing him and Antoine. Because of their military background, they had several enemies.

The sheriff expelled a ragged sigh of resignation. "The danger could follow you home. It probably is better that you all stay where I can protect you."

Sebastian chuckled. "As I said, Sheriff, I will protect myself as well as the witness. I will wait here until she arrives to claim her reward for the information she's been withholding."

"You could have a long wait," Wolf warned. "It may already be too late for that witness."

IT WASN'T TOO LATE. She could turn around and head to the Wind River Ranch and Resort to collect that last check, like she had intended. But instead Jessica steered the Suburban around a couple of television station vans that still lined the street. Even though it had been a few hours since the prince's press conference, they remained outside the three-story beige brick county courthouse that housed the sheriff's office. Was he still here?

She maneuvered the ranch vehicle into an empty space quite a ways down the block. Then she glanced at the cell phone she'd dropped onto the passenger seat. Why had she called? Because of his damned eyes, imploring her to do the right thing. But was this the right thing?

If one of the camera crew captured her on film and nationally broadcast the coverage…

Would he recognize her? She glanced into the rearview mirror and even after nearly five years of this auburn color and long, straight style, she barely recognized herself except for her eyes. She could have tried to hide the brown with colored contacts, but she wouldn't have been able to hide the fear that she'd never stopped feeling. Not with him out there, determined to find her.

And kill her.

But it wasn't just her life she risked by coming here. She could be risking the sheik's, too. What if he was safer if no one knew he was alive? But she remembered the anguish and frustration in Prince Sebastian

Cavanaugh's blue gaze, and guilt churned in her stomach. He had to know what had happened to his friend. She had to tell him.

Her fingers trembling, she fumbled with the handle before opening the driver's door and sliding out of the vehicle. Then, head down, she hurried past the reporters' vans. She hesitated outside the county courthouse before pushing open the door and stepping inside. Security scanners blocked the foyer, but while she stepped into a line, she could see into the outer office where the conference had been held. A few reporters waited while cameramen filmed the deputies taking calls.

Were those calls coming from people trying to claim the reward? But no one else had seen what she had, except for whoever she'd spied driving away from the scene. Maybe that person had decided to come forward and Jessica didn't need to be here; she didn't need to risk her own safety. Or Samantha's.

She stepped out of the security line and backed toward the doors. She couldn't risk going inside with all those cameras. But before she could turn away, Prince Sebastian looked up from the desk over which he'd been leaning. And his deep blue gaze met hers.

Panic accelerated her pulse, so that it leaped at her throat and hammered at her wrists. Even though several feet and people separated them, she had confirmation that the television screen had not made him more handsome than reality. With his golden brown hair, those piercing eyes and his long, lean body, he was as handsome in person as he'd been on the screen. More so even. Heat flashed through her along with the panic.

But then a camera flashed and another lens turned toward her, and panic won out. She turned and ran. But the sick feeling in her stomach warned her that it was already too late. Coming here had been a mistake. One that would probably get her killed.

Chapter Two

When the redhead turned and ran, breaking that strange connection between them, Sebastian's breath shuddered out. Then, after those breathless seconds that he'd held perfectly still when their gazes had met, he moved again. Shoving through the security screeners, he pushed open the doors to the courthouse and raced after her.

She had to be the witness because he'd glimpsed the fear in her dark eyes, which had widened when the cameras had turned on her. The reporters hadn't missed his interest in the woman who'd entered the courthouse but hesitated at the screeners. Sebastian had wanted to draw out the witness, not just for information about his friend but also to warn her.

Apparently she didn't need his warning; she already knew she was in danger. And she ran as if an assassin—not a prince—pursued her. Despite his legs being longer than hers, he had to run to catch her. She'd already jumped inside her rusted SUV, but he grabbed the door before she could swing it closed.

"Let me go!" she implored him, her voice cracking with fear.

He shook his head. "You cannot leave until you say what you came here to tell me."

"I—I didn't come here to talk to you."

"You are not the one who called and asked if I was at the office?"

Color suffused her delicately featured face. "No— No, that wasn't me."

He would not need Antoine's assistance to determine if she spoke the truth or lies. She was not a very good liar. "Then why were you coming into the courthouse?"

"Uh, I have a ticket to pay."

"You left before you paid it," he pointed out.

"I—I forgot my checkbook."

"Show me the citation," he challenged her.

The color in her cheeks deepened to a darker red, nearly the same shade as her long auburn hair. "I forgot that, too."

"You're quite forgetful," he mused. "Is that why you haven't come forward before?"

Breaking the connection of their gazes, she ducked her head. "I don't know what you're talking about. I just got that ticket."

"That will be easy enough to verify with Sheriff Wolf. What is your name?"

She tugged on the door handle. "You don't need to verify anything. Just let me leave."

"Not until you share with me what you saw that

night." Had Amir survived the explosion or had someone removed his body to conceal his murder? But that made no sense. Why leave the chauffeur's burned corpse and remove Amir's?

Of course, none of it made sense. They had come to the United States to propose trade agreements that would benefit this country as well as COIN, especially the methods Prince Stefan Lutece had developed to make oil drilling environmentally safe. These methods were the only reason that Sebastian and Antoine had agreed to drill on Barajas, but they needed a buyer for that oil. They needed money for health care and other social services, so nobody else left their island for Europe or America. And so that the voice inside his head wouldn't keep telling him that he wasn't cut out to be a ruler or a protector.

"Tell me what you saw," he demanded, his frustration gnawing away at his usually rigid control.

She flinched but stubbornly repeated, "I don't know what you're talking about."

"You cannot claim the reward until you share your eyewitness account of the explosion."

"I don't want a reward."

"Of course you do," he said, dismissing her claim. "That is why you came here. And why you wanted to make certain I would be here when you arrived—to collect your money." Not to ambush him as the sheriff had warned. Of course, if that had been her plan, he had stepped neatly into her trap when he'd raced after her. But when their gazes had met and held, he'd felt no threat from her—only *to* her.

She shook her head, and her hair nearly brushed the shoulder of his suit because he stood so close to her— close enough to smell her summer fresh outdoors scent. "I don't want your money."

He held in a snort of derision, not wanting to offend her despite his anger over her taking so long to come forward. She obviously had more pride than money. The color of her vehicle was indiscernible from the rust eating away at the metal. Her clothes had also seen better days. Her jeans were torn, her dimpled knees peaking through the holes in the washed-out denim. The cuffs and collar of her blue plaid blouse were frayed, the mismatched buttons straining across her full breasts.

Awareness raised the dark hairs on his forearms and heated his stomach. Despite her threadbare attire, she was an attractive woman—beautiful even with her wide, brown eyes and delicate features. But stubborn, too. No matter how much she denied it, she needed his money.

He glanced around her and checked out the inside of her vehicle. The seats were torn, foam protruding through the rips in the upholstery. The headliner hung low, separated from the roof. But it was what he noticed in the back that drew his attention. Some kind of booster-type car seat was buckled into a seat, empty for now. But she must have a child, unless she'd borrowed someone else's vehicle. "Are you a mother?"

She followed his gaze, her breath audibly catching. "That's not any of your business."

He focused on her left hand that clutched the door handle. The fingers were bare but for scrapes and calluses. That didn't mean she wasn't married with children. She might have just removed her ring because of the manual labor she obviously did. He ignored the disappointment that cooled the heat in his stomach.

His attraction to her was ridiculous anyway. He dated only princesses and heiresses—women clad in designer gowns, not ragged jeans. Women who wore jewels, not calluses. As Grandfather had constantly lectured him and Antoine, princes could marry only princesses and vice versa. King Omar had practiced what he'd preached; he'd married the princess of a small European country lost during a civil war, and he'd brought her to reign over Barajas with him. If only their princess mother had listened to her father and married a prince instead of a mercenary...

He needed to make this woman listen to him. "What you witnessed makes you my business." That was the only reason for his interest in her.

"I didn't witness anything. I don't want your reward. I just want to leave," she said, her voice shaky with frustration and that fear she wasn't able to conceal.

"If you don't want my money," he said, carefully hiding his skepticism, "then how about my protection?"

"Protection?" she asked, her eyes widening as she stared up at him.

"Is that not why you didn't come forward earlier—because you were too frightened?" And perhaps not just for her own safety but also for the child she might have, if that car seat belonged to her. From her reaction, he was almost certain that it did. So she had a child. But did she have a husband? He suspected not because if she had someone to protect her, she should not be so scared. "You need not be afraid."

She didn't hold in her snort but expelled it softly.

He lifted his chin, offended at her derision. He was a ruler—coruler—and a former military officer. How dare she doubt him and remind him of someone else in his life who always had? "I will protect you."

JESSICA LAUGHED. She need not be afraid? She couldn't remember a time when she hadn't been afraid. "You can't protect me."

No one could.

"Have you already been threatened?" he asked, his voice deepening with concern. "Is that why you haven't reported what you've seen?"

She had other reasons for not reporting, like that relentless media coverage. Had any of those reporters followed them out? Had they caught her image on camera? Even before the explosion, the coverage of the COIN summit had been national—broadcast on every network to every city. She'd tried hard to avoid the cameras every time she came to town or went to the Wind River Ranch and Resort. Until today she was pretty positive she'd been successful.

To see if the reporters had followed her like the prince had, she tried to look out the driver's door, but she couldn't see beyond him. He was too big. Too broad. Too close, so close that with every breath she drew, she inhaled him. He even smelled like a prince: regal and rich—musk and leather and a faint trace of citrus. His scent filled her lungs and had her heart pounding furiously. "I—I have to go."

"You're not leaving until you tell me what you saw that night," he ordered as if she were one of his subjects or his servants.

She was certain that would be the only relationship he'd ever entertain with someone like her. He'd boss her around and bully her—just like…

"I can't stay!" she said, her panic escaping in a squeak that cracked her voice.

Those reporters couldn't have missed how he'd chased after her. Even though she couldn't see beyond his broad shoulders, she was certain that they had followed him. They would have to follow the story. She shouldn't have come here—shouldn't have let his blue eyes persuade her to risk everything for him. To ease his fear for his friend, she'd confronted hers. Why?

He was nothing more to her than a handsome stranger. And a stranger was all he could ever be.

She tugged harder on the handle, but the door didn't budge. He held tight to the edge of the rusted metal.

With her right hand, she jammed the key in the ignition, and with a silent prayer that it would start the first time, she turned the motor. The engine miraculously roared to life, the Suburban shuddering from the high idle and the missing exhaust.

"What are you doing?" the prince demanded, shouting to be heard over the motor.

She slammed the transmission into Drive and stepped on the gas, pulling away with the door hanging open. The metal slipped through the prince's grasp. He ran, as if trying to leap inside the vehicle with her, but she accelerated. Then, with her hand shaking, she slammed the door shut.

She spared him only a glance in her rearview mirror. Standing in a cloud of exhaust, he stared after her as if dumbstruck that she had disobeyed him and that she had escaped him. For now. The sick feeling in the pit of her stomach warned her that he would be just as relentless as that other man in tracking down her.

"WHAT THE HELL—"

Sebastian echoed the sheriff's sentiments as the man joined him in the street. What the hell had just happened?

"—were you thinking!" Wolf yelled. "Running after her like that, you could have been running right into her trap."

"She didn't trap me." Except in her gaze, with her fear and vulnerability.

"She freaked at the courthouse's security screening," Wolf said. "Most likely because she was armed. You're lucky you didn't get your damn head blown off."

Sebastian's temper flared; he did not like being reprimanded like a child or a fool even though he had to acknowledge that he might have acted like one. The fear in the woman's eyes had brought out his protective instincts so that he'd worried only about her safety and not his own.

"She was not armed," Sebastian insisted. Or more than likely she would have pulled the gun on him to get him to leave her alone.

"The sheriff is right, Your Highness." Brenner, the head of the Barajas security detail, said. "You should not have left the courthouse without our protection."

"I am fine," Sebastian insisted, even though his pulse raced just like she had raced away from him. "Or I will be when I find her."

"She is the witness?" Wolf asked.

Sebastian nodded.

"Did she tell you what she saw?" Brenner asked.

"Not yet," he replied. "The reporters frightened her off with their cameras."

"That's why I had my deputies detain them," Wolf said, his mouth curving into a slight grin as he glanced back toward the courthouse.

"I thought you didn't believe she was the witness," Sebastian said. "You were concerned that she might be another hired assassin."

"And if that had been the case, I didn't need any more collateral damage in Wind River County."

"There has been quite enough," Sebastian agreed. "I need to find her so that we can prevent something happening to anyone else. I need to learn what she saw." He needed to know if Amir lived or...

The sheriff rubbed his hand along his jaw as if struggling with something. Then, with a sigh, he admitted, "I know where you can find her."

"Where?"

"The Double J. That's who the plate is registered to."

He had been talking to her long enough for the sheriff to run the plate, and still he had not convinced her to tell him the truth. "Where is the Double J?"

"It's about halfway between the Wind River Ranch and Resort and the Rattlesnake Badlands on Snake Valley Road, the same road where the limo exploded."

Sebastian turned toward Brenner and held out his hand. "Give me your keys."

"Your Highness, I will drive you."

He shook his head. "No, I cannot risk anyone else frightening her off."

"But she could still be—doing as the sheriff suggested—setting a trap for you."

"She is not going to ambush me." He feared she had something almost as bad planned, though. "Instead, she's going to run away." Flee, before she told him what she'd seen that night. "I order you to turn over your keys. Now."

Unable to ignore a direct order, Brenner, his hand shaking, dropped the keys into Sebastian's palm. "But, Your Highness—"

Ignoring the security detail's concern, Sebastian rushed off toward the black Hummer parked directly outside the courthouse, behind the sheriff's white Dodge SUV. Sebastian had already wasted precious minutes arguing with these men and had lost miles of road to her. After gunning the engine, he pressed hard on the accelerator, determined to close the distance between them.

But the traffic in town had him slowing and steering around other vehicles. Several minutes and more miles passed until he neared the drive leading to the resort. He sped past the turnoff for the resort and traffic thinned to just one vehicle ahead of him—a white panel van. Like a snake, the road wound through the lush valley, and at a curve, he caught a glimpse of the rusted SUV just ahead of the van. He accelerated and steered to the left, to pass the van. But it sped up and veered across the line, cutting him off.

He hit the brakes and cursed.

"What's wrong?" The question, and the familiar voice, emanated from a speaker inside the visor. The vehicle was equipped with a hands-free communication system.

"Brenner called you," he said, surmising that the head of the Barajas security detail had notified his twin that he'd gone rogue. Or even more rogue. When they'd discovered that the bomb had been meant to kill them all, they'd gone into seclusion at the resort. Well, almost all of them had. Sheik Efraim Aziz had insisted on personally searching for Amir. Sebastian had already been taking a risk holding the press conference in town, and for him to now go off alone with the threat against them...

"Brenner's worried that you're going to get yourself killed," Antoine replied.

"Are *you?*" Sebastian tried again to pass the van, but it veered back across the line, blocking his maneuver.

"Should I be?"

Sebastian grinned despite his frustration with the van. "You know me too well to worry about me."

"It is because I know you so well that I worry," Antoine replied. "Come by the resort, and I will ride with you out to the Double J ranch."

"I have already passed the resort." And if he didn't pass the van, he might miss the driveway for the ranch. Why the hell would the van not let him by?

"Turn around," Antoine commanded. "Knowing that we are all in danger, you should not have gone off alone."

"I'm not alone," Sebastian murmured as he studied the van through eyes narrowed in suspicion.

"Who's with you? You left Brenner stranded at the Wind River courthouse."

"I'm not alone on the road," he clarified. Why wasn't he? If the street was as remote as the sheriff's report had led him to believe… "There is a van between my vehicle and the witness's."

The road curved again, and Sebastian caught a glimpse of the rusted Suburban and the red-haired woman in the driver's seat who tightly gripped the steering wheel. Had she seen his vehicle behind the van? Seeing the van was probably enough to frighten her. Who the hell was in it? Reporters? With no windows on the sides, just sliding panels, it looked similar to the many vans that had been parked outside the courthouse.

He edged closer again, nearly pushing his grill against the back bumper. "Have the sheriff run this plate…" Mud had been smeared across it, concealing the numbers.

"What is it?" Antoine asked.

"Can't read it." He swerved to the left so quickly that the van didn't have time to cut him off. But it tried, banging hard against the side of the Hummer. The metal of the van crumpled. There was no station name or number on the side of it, either. "Damn…"

"What?" Antoine asked.

"I don't think they are reporters." He pushed harder on the gas, surging the Hummer forward until he'd drawn level with the driver's window of the van. But the glass was so heavily tinted that he could not see through it.

"Back off," Antoine advised him.

Instead of heeding his brother's advice, Sebastian cranked the steering wheel and slammed the Hummer into the van, just as they had slammed into him. Metal crunched and tires squealed. The seat belt snapped against his neck and chest as the impact jostled him. Both vehicles spun out, gravel spewing as they skidded off the pavement onto the shoulder of the winding road.

"What the hell's going on?" Antoine's shout vibrated in the speaker.

Reaching beneath the seat for Brenner's spare weapon, the one he would not have been able to get through the security screeners, Sebastian assured his twin, "I have it under control."

"Wait for me," Antoine implored him. "I can be there shortly with a few of the security detail."

"You'll be too late," Sebastian replied as he pushed open the driver's door. Dirt swirled in the wind, stinging his eyes, so he had to squint against it and the sunlight as he approached the van.

The heavily tinted window lowered just a couple of inches—not enough for Sebastian to see the driver. All he caught was a glimpse—a glint, really—of sunshine off metal.

He was not the only one who was armed. Perhaps he should have worn a bulletproof vest for the press conference as Antoine and the sheriff had suggested. But if a true marksman had been hired to kill them, Sebastian knew they always went for the head shot.

Chapter Three

Gravel spewed as the van slammed into reverse. The tires fishtailed off the shoulder and then back onto the road. The prince stood in the cloud of dust swirling around him, a gun—probably a GLOCK—gripped tightly in his hand.

Dmitri held on to his own weapon, the barrel of the Ruger revolver trained on the prince as the driver continued backing away from the Hummer. "I should have fired at him," he grumbled. "I still have a shot." But only for a few more moments as the distance between them widened.

"Prince Sebastian is not the intended target," the driver, Nic, reminded him. "We do not have clearance to kill him."

"Not yet." Dmitri reluctantly holstered his gun. Then he reached for his cell, his hand shaking slightly as anger coursed through him. "But we will…"

"The son of a bitch ran us off the road," Nic snapped as his anger erupted.

"Ran *you* off the road." Had Dmitri been driving, that

would not have happened. He punched in a speed-dial number and swallowed hard when the boss answered immediately.

"Is it?" the man asked.

"We were not able to get close enough to tell," Dmitri admitted.

"Why not?"

"We had interference," he reluctantly explained, "from one of the royals."

"Which one?"

"The one who held the press conference offering the reward. Prince Sebastian Cavanaugh. I had a shot. Should I have taken it?" Dmitri asked, turning to glare at the driver.

A deep chuckle emanated from the phone. "The *prince* is no threat."

"He has military experience." Dmitri recalled learning from the conference. He had posed as one of the reporters and then hung around with them afterward on the off chance that she might come forward for that reward. The prince had done what they had not been able to. He'd drawn her out of hiding.

"A prince with any *real* military experience?" The boss snorted. "I'm sure he never left his barracks without his security detail. He is no threat."

"But we lost our tail on her because of him," Dmitri said. Despite his efforts, Nic had been unable to keep the Hummer from passing them. Was it because, as Nic had grumbled, the Hummer was just more powerful than the van? Or was it because the prince was more powerful than Nic or the boss would admit?

"The plan was to use him to find her," the boss reminded him. "Follow the plan. Follow the prince. He'll lead you to her."

"And once we have her?"

A chuckle rattled over the cell phone. "Then you will kill Prince Sebastian Cavanaugh, of course."

"Of course…"

Dmitri stared through the dust-smeared windshield at the Hummer in the distance. As the prince rounded the rear of the vehicle to approach the driver's side, sunlight glinted off the weapon he held.

Maybe the boss was right. Maybe the prince's military experience meant nothing. But the tightening muscles in Dmitri's gut told him that when the time came, Prince Sebastian Cavanaugh might not be all that easy to kill.

WITH HANDS TREMBLING, Jessica slid the dead bolt closed. Then she peered through the sheer curtain over the window in the door. Nothing had pulled into the dirt driveway behind the Suburban, but there had been vehicles following her. First the van. Probably the reporters from the sheriff's office.

She shuddered at the thought of their cameras catching her on film to be broadcast everywhere…

She'd also heard another engine—one more powerful than the van's. Then the crunch of metal grinding against metal had echoed throughout the valley. Due to the winding road, she hadn't caught a glimpse of an accident in her rearview mirror—unlike the night of the explosion when the flames and wreckage had been unavoidable. She wished she hadn't seen what she had that night. So today she hadn't been about to stop to find out what had happened or even to find out who was following her.

She was damn sure she knew to whom one of those vehicles belonged. Prince Sebastian. Had he been involved in a crash?

A pang of concern stabbed her heart, and she gasped. While she didn't trust him, she would hate for him to be hurt—not because she personally cared what happened to him, though. She just hated the thought of anyone getting hurt.

Except one man.

"Someone follow you back from the resort?" Helen asked, peering over Jessica's shoulder.

She sucked in a breath. "Where's Samantha?"

"In her room, cleaning up like you told her. She's such a good kid—always minds her mama," Helen said with so much pride that she could have been the little girl's biological grandmother instead of just her honorary one.

Her breath escaped in a ragged sigh. "If only I'd do what I tell myself to do..."

Helen chuckled. "You're a good girl, too, Jessica. What are you talking about?"

"I didn't go to the resort," she admitted.

"You went to town."

Choking on regrets, she could only nod.

Helen squeezed her shoulders. "That was a lot of money."

"I didn't collect it," she said. "I didn't tell him anything." Sure, the prince had seemed genuinely concerned about his friend, but she knew too well that concern— even love—could be faked to mask someone's true nature or agenda.

"So that's why you're worried he followed you back here?" Helen asked, continuing to stare down the long gravel driveway. It was so long that they couldn't see the road, though. Someone could have turned off behind her, and she would not know.

"I don't think he was the only one following me," she said. "I'm sorry."

"For what?"

"For bringing trouble back to the ranch."

"I don't see any cars out there, honey." Helen stepped back. "You must have lost them."

"For now," Jessica said, turning away from the door. "But someone in town might have recognized the Suburban, and if he—or anyone else—asks around…"

"They'll know where to find you."

"At the Double J. I knew Samantha and I would have to leave here someday, but I'd hoped to do that before I brought trouble to you." She shouldn't have stayed in one place for so long. When she'd first run away, she hadn't stayed anywhere for more than a few weeks. But then she'd had Samantha, and the little girl had needed a home. "After everything you've done for me, that's the last thing I ever intended to do."

Helen shrugged off Jessica's concern. "Because the bottom of the *J* rotted off, it's the double *T*. Double Trouble, honey. Trouble's been here long before you showed up in Wind River County. Trouble will end here, too."

That was what Jessica was afraid of…

"So the van's gone?" Antoine asked, his voice sharp with frustration as it emanated from the speaker.

"It took off." He shouldn't have let it, but he'd had no justification for shooting out the tires or windows. So he'd refrained from firing his weapon, even though his finger had itched to pull the trigger.

Hell, he'd probably had no justification for running the van off the road in the first place. Sure, it hadn't let him pass, but drivers in the States were different than drivers in Barajas. There was road rage here. And there was also royal rage here in Wind River. Perhaps they had recognized the Hummer as belonging to COIN security detail and that was why they'd driven as erratically as they had. But Sebastian suspected the driver hadn't acted out of road or royal rage but had had another agenda entirely.

Plan B?

Prince Stefan Lutece had learned from a forensics

expert that the bomb had been intended for all of them and that when it had failed, whoever was behind the assassination attempt had moved on to plan B. Whatever that was…

"You probably scared the hell out of some reporters," Antoine remarked.

"I hope."

"I'm sure they'll leave her alone now."

Sebastian seriously doubted that they would leave the woman alone or that they were just reporters. When the window had rolled down a crack, sunshine had glinted off the metal of the barrel of a gun. Even though he'd more often stared down the barrel of a long-range sniper rifle, he had recognized when he'd been staring into one.

"If they were reporters, they would have asked me for a statement, would they not? Reporters have been hounding us since we arrived in Wyoming. I was alone. They could have asked me whatever questions they wanted." Instead they had flashed a gun and then had driven away in reverse to escape him.

"Even alone you're not exactly approachable," Antoine said with a teasing chuckle. "And if they weren't reporters but some of the hired guns, wouldn't they have done something else to you…because you were alone? You'd presented them with a great opportunity."

"But perhaps they are not after me."

"Even before there was a hit put out on the witness, that bomb had been set in the limo to take out *all* of us,"

Antoine bitterly reminded him. "If there were hit men in that van, they would have gone after you."

Sebastian expelled a breath of relief. "Of course. You're right." He chuckled. "So I did scare the hell out of some reporters."

"As you said, they've been hounding us since we arrived—they had it coming."

"They had it coming for interfering in my following the witness. I think I lost her," he admitted. "The sheriff said her vehicle was registered to the Double J, but the only ranch I've found between the resort and the Rattlesnake Badlands is the Double T." When he'd reached the badlands, he'd turned around and headed back to the driveway to that ranch. As he drove past it, he glanced at the wooden sign that hung on rusted chains from a sawed-off log. The *T* looked odd. Perhaps it had once been a *J*. But if it hadn't, he could ask if anyone knew where he could find the Double J.

And the witness…

The dirt drive wound between fenced pastures and past a couple of weathered red barns to a two-story farmhouse. He wouldn't need to ask where to find the Double J; he'd found it. He parked behind the rusted SUV. "I'm here," he told his brother.

"You found the witness."

"She's here."

"Wait for me before you approach her again," Antoine urged. "You shouldn't be out—anywhere—alone."

"I'll be fine. Her vehicle is the only one here." Unless

there was one parked inside one of those big barns. To be careful, and because he couldn't shake the experience with the van, he carried the gun he'd pulled from beneath the seat. He'd tucked it in the waistband of his pants and covered it with his suit jacket. Ever since they'd learned of the threat to their lives, he'd carried a weapon or had one stashed within reach.

When he'd finished out his service in the military, Sebastian had sworn to never take up a weapon again. But then he hadn't considered that he'd ever have to go back to war. While it wasn't official yet, that explosion had been a declaration of war—or at least the first battle. Had Amir survived it?

"Not seeing another vehicle doesn't mean much," Antoine spoke as he often did, as if he was privy to Sebastian's thoughts. That damn twin connection of theirs.

Sebastian glanced back down the long driveway, making sure no one had followed him, but he couldn't see to the road. Someone could have followed him that far and headed back to the ranch on foot now.

"She's by herself," he said. Unless she had a husband. But then why had the man let her go into town alone when she was already aware that she was in danger? Why hadn't he been there to protect her?

Sebastian pushed open the driver's door and stepped onto the drive. "I'll let you know what I find out," he assured his brother.

"Be careful," Antoine advised.

"I'll be fine. Don't worry, you won't have to rule Barajas alone."

A vulgar curse shot out of the speaker.

Sebastian chuckled at his brother's name-calling as he slammed the door shut. His brother had a tendency to be overprotective of him but with good reason. They had been all that each other had for a long time now. And they, as well as the other royals, were in mortal danger right now.

Along with the witness.

He crossed the porch to the front door, and a curtain twitched at a window. Not wanting to scare her any more, he brushed his knuckles softly against the weathered wood. A shadow moved behind that curtain.

"It is all right," he assured her. "I came alone. You are not in any danger."

Just to make certain no one had walked up from the road, he glanced around him toward the barns and pastures. While he stared away, the door creaked open behind him; she must have finally decided to trust him.

He turned back, and this time he had no doubt that he was staring into the barrel of a gun. Actually the *double* barrel of a shotgun.

Despite the fear Sebastian had been convinced he'd seen in her eyes, she wasn't in any danger.

But he sure as hell was. It appeared as though Sheriff Wolf had been right. With her wide vulnerable eyes and sexy little body, the mysterious red-haired woman had lured him right into her trap.

Perhaps she'd been telling him the truth, too, when she'd denied seeing anything the night of the explosion. Apparently she wasn't the witness with a hit out on her. She was a hired assassin about to carry out the hit on him.

Chapter Four

While her heart pounded furiously with the fear coursing through her, Jessica steadied her hands on the shotgun, so that he couldn't pull the weapon from her grasp. But he didn't reach for it. Instead he propped his fists on his lean hips and stared her down just as he had the pushy reporters during the press conference.

She resisted the urge to squirm beneath that stare. She refused to be intimidated. Again. By his manner—or his looks.

Why did he have to be so damn handsome? That golden brown hair, those deep blue eyes and his long, lean body clad in a dark suit—all conspired to addle a woman's brains. Jessica would not be addled, either.

Summoning her pride and whatever strength she possessed, she lifted her chin and met his stare of intimidation head-on. Those damn mesmerizing eyes of his narrowed as he scrutinized her face as if he could see right inside her mind. Or her heart. Or her soul.

"Put down the gun," he ordered as if she were one of

his subjects or servants. Then he lowered his voice and softly added, "Before you hurt yourself."

Was he for real?

She'd expected him to be furious with her for driving off as she had, with him nearly being dragged along with her vehicle. When he'd spouted that nonsense about her not being in any danger before she'd opened the door, she'd figured he had to be lying. Men always lied to her. Even though he was a prince, he was a man first.

"I'm not the one who's going to get hurt if you don't leave me alone," she warned him, shoving the barrel closer to his chest.

His gaze dropped from hers to the gun, then rose back up to her face. But he still didn't move. Despite her holding a weapon on him, he betrayed no fear.

Jealousy flashed through her—along with wistful admiration. Even after the explosion and attempts on the lives of the other royals, he felt no fear. Jessica couldn't remember a time when she hadn't been afraid. But maybe it was good that she had enough sense to get scared; it had probably kept her alive for the past five years.

"I wasn't wrong," he murmured, as if talking only to himself. Then he raised his voice and added, "You're not going to shoot me."

His arrogance and condescension grated on her already frayed nerves.

"I will if you don't leave. You're trespassing," she informed him. "Get off this property."

He remained standing stubbornly right in front of her—as if she hadn't spoken at all. "I am not leaving until you tell me what you saw that night."

She pressed the barrel against the lapel on the left side of his dark suit jacket, and finally, he stepped back. She followed him onto the porch and pulled the door closed behind herself. When the Hummer had come down the driveway, Helen had joined Samantha in her room to make sure the little girl stayed upstairs and at the back of the house. But Jessica didn't want his voice—or hers—to drift up within the child's hearing.

Even though she'd only had one hand on the old shotgun when she'd shut the door, he hadn't tried to pull it from her. So she observed, "You're smart enough to know to not grab for the gun."

He lifted his chin, as if offended. "I know how dangerous guns can be."

Of course. According to Danny Harold, Prince Sebastian Cavanaugh had been a military sniper. "Then you should also be smart enough to leave. You're wasting your time anyway. I have *nothing* to tell you."

He flinched, as if worried that by *nothing* she meant that his friend was dead. And once again that anguish and frustration passed through his deep blue eyes. But she suspected his frustration wasn't just over not knowing where his friend was but with her for not telling him what he wanted to know.

Because she'd expected him to be angry with her, she'd greeted him with the shotgun. No man would ever hurt her again. But she didn't want to hurt him, either. She didn't lower the gun, however. With Samantha in the house, she could not let the man any closer.

He was already too close. His nearness had her skin heating and tingling and her pulse racing with awareness. She could not be attracted to him.

She couldn't...

But she could tell him about that night. She could ease his worry. If she could trust him...

"I know that you're frightened," he said, his deep voice low and soft. "But you have nothing to fear from me. I will protect you from harm. The people who caused the explosion will not get to you."

She couldn't trust him. She had learned long ago that men who made promises that were impossible to keep were not to be trusted.

SEBASTIAN HAD LOST HER. Even though she stood right there in front of him, she was gone. For a moment she had appeared about to confide in him. Her gaze had warmed and she'd relaxed her grip on the gun.

But now she clutched the shotgun tightly, the stock braced against her slender shoulder as if she were preparing to fire on him. And the brief warming of her brown eyes had cooled.

Disappointment clenched the muscles in his stomach and not just because she wouldn't tell him about the explosion. He was disappointed that her warmth was gone, and that she was all tense and scared again. He hated that she was so afraid and not just for her sake. Her fear brought him back to a dark place he'd never wanted to go again.

"Let me help you," he urged.

When she had first greeted him with the gun, he'd thought for a moment that she might intend to shoot him and collect the money that someone had put on his head along with the other royals. But that moment had been fleeting. He'd had only to look into her eyes to know that she was no killer. He didn't want her to become a victim, either.

"You don't want to help me," she replied. "You want me to help you." She shook her head. "And I can't…"

"You could," he said, "if you'd let yourself trust me."

The color drained from her face, leaving her too pale and fragile looking. "I can't…"

"My nation—Barajas—trusts me and my brother to rule them and to protect them."

That was the whole point of the summit, to recharge their economy and gain them powerful allies. If Grandfather lived, he might have even approved of the trade agreement, although that was unlikely; King Omar had approved of so little his grandsons had done—mostly because he had not approved of what they were. Half commoner.

"If an entire nation can trust me," he asked, "why can't you?"

"Some leaders are ruthless," she said. "They use

intimidation and violence to rule." From the way she stared up at him, her eyes wide and dark with fear, she believed he was that kind of ruler.

"I would never…"

She took one hand from the gun to reach behind her and open the door. He could have grabbed the shotgun from her—probably with no risk of it going off because her fingers were not near the trigger. But what would he do then—threaten her with it to tell him what he wanted to know? She was already too afraid to talk; scaring her more would not convince her to trust him.

"You would never what?" she asked, as if interested in what he'd left unsaid.

He'd been about to say that he would never resort to violence. But that wasn't true because he had. In the military, during battle. Since coming to America, he'd felt as if he was at war again and that he had to be prepared for an attack from every direction.

Friend and foe.

And here this woman stood with double barrels pointed at his chest, threatening to pull the trigger. Obviously she, too, knew something about needing to be prepared for an attack.

"I would never hurt you," he assured her.

Her stubborn jaw eased slightly as her lips parted on a wistful sigh, as if she wanted to believe him but dared not. The vulnerability in her dark eyes compelled him to reach out—not for the gun but to her face. But when his hand neared her cheek, she flinched.

He pulled his hand back to his side but fisted it, wanting to slam it into the face of whoever had hurt her. After her reaction, he realized he was too late to protect her. She had already been someone's victim.

"Have you been threatened?" he asked. "Has whoever is behind the explosion already found you?" Perhaps that person had put the fear of God in her to keep quiet about what she'd seen that night.

She shook her head, tumbling that thick red hair around her shoulders. But now, standing as close as he was to her, he could tell that the roots were not red but a deep chocolate brown. Why would she have dyed such rich, silky-looking hair? To hide?

"Have you been found?" he asked again, as concern for her safety—and the safety of the child who used that car seat—filled him. That child was probably why she'd guarded the door and the house, so that he would not see her kid. Or so that her kid would not see him.

"No," she said. "But I will be found…if you don't leave me alone."

"Yes, you will," he agreed, remembering the van that had followed her from the courthouse. "That's why you and your child need to come with me, so that I can protect you both."

She shook her head again, unwilling and perhaps unable to believe him.

"Tell me what you saw that night," he implored her.

"I didn't say that I saw anything," she said.

"You didn't," he replied. "In fact you've denied it until you admitted that they're going to find you."

"Because you're here," she said, her voice rising with frustration. "Because you're convinced I'm the witness, you're going to wind up convincing them—whoever they are—that I am."

Was that true? Had he put her more at risk than she'd already been? Then that made him even more responsible for her safety, and as a prince, he took his responsibilities very seriously. Too many people depended on him.

"Once you share what you know, you will no longer be a threat," he pointed out.

As she had outside the sheriff's office, she snorted her derision. "I am not a threat now."

"And once you tell me what you saw, I will give you that reward." Hell, he would give her more than he'd offered. "It's enough money that you can go far away from here. You can get away from whoever these people are." And whoever else had made it so difficult for her to trust.

"Right now, I just want to get away from you," she said. And she slammed the door between them. The bolt slid into place, locking him out.

This woman had threatened his life twice. First, when she had driven off and nearly dragged him along with her vehicle. And second, when she'd thrust a gun in his face and then pressed the barrel against his chest.

But he felt no anger for her—only an overwhelming

sense of protection. Maybe there had been just reporters in that van, but he couldn't take the chance that they had been. He couldn't take the chance that they or whoever else had hurt her wouldn't find her. And hurt her again.

"Is HE GONE?" Jessica asked as she carried a box down the stairs.

Helen turned away from the window. "I don't see his fancy SUV anymore."

"That doesn't mean he's not still out there." Watching. She had been watched for so long…until she'd finally escaped and started a new life. A life she now had to give up.

"I take it that you didn't tell him what he wants to know," Helen mused as she took the box from Jessica's arms and set it with the others piled near the door.

"I can't risk it," Jessica replied—even though her stomach clenched into knots over that anguish she'd glimpsed in his compelling eyes. She'd wanted to tell him about his friend. But what if he was not really a friend to the man from the explosion? What if he was a threat?

"I don't know who's a good guy or who's a bad guy." She had never been able to tell that—until it was too late.

"I just know that I have to get out of here. Now." Before the most dangerous man she'd ever known found her and Samantha.

Maybe she should have taken the prince's reward and taken his advice to go far away. But if she'd revealed what she'd seen that night, it wouldn't have been just her life she risked. And she didn't know if that other person affected had had the time or the resources to get far, far away from danger.

"Then you'll need this." Helen pressed some crumpled bills into Jessica's hand.

"I can't take your money," she protested, thrusting the wad back at her. "You need all of it to keep the Double J going, so that someday you can turn it into a shelter like you've always wanted to." But in a way Helen had turned it into one already, when she'd offered Jessica shelter four years ago. Helen had recognized Jessica not for her real identify but for what she was—on the run from an abusive relationship. Helen had recognized her because she'd seen herself and her old fears in Jessica. She, too, had escaped an abusive relationship. She'd survived—but her husband hadn't because Helen had no compunction against pulling the trigger to protect herself.

"I want to do that because I want to help women who need help," Helen said. "You need help, Jessica, so let me help you."

Prince Sebastian had offered to help her, too, but with ulterior motives that Jessica could not trust. Helen offered because she was a true friend. The best one Jessica had ever had and leaving her and the Double J—the only home Samantha had ever known—would be so hard.

Tears stung Jessica's eyes, and she blinked furiously to fight them back. She couldn't cry. Not now.

"You can help me," she said. "You can watch Samantha for me again while I pick up my last check."

"You're really going to the Wind River Ranch this time?" Helen asked, skeptically arching a gray brow.

"Yes."

"You'll probably run into him," Helen warned. "That's no doubt where he's gone now. All the royals are staying at the resort."

All but one.

Jessica nodded. "I know that."

Everyone in the world knew where they were staying, at the luxurious resort on hundreds of acres in Wind River County.

"But I'm going in the back employee entrance," she said. "I won't see him there." With the expansive size of the lodge and ranch, she was unlikely to run into him again.

She couldn't run into him again because if she did, she would probably tell him what she had seen that horrible night when the limo had exploded in flames, bits of metal and glass flying through the darkness.

But to share what she'd seen wouldn't risk just her life. That other man from the explosion might have only survived because no one knew for certain that he had. If he didn't trust his royal friends, why should she?

Chapter Five

The red-headed woman moved within the small circle of the scope. He adjusted the lens, so he could see her up close. The wind ruffled her hair, tousling the strands, so that the deep brown shone through the auburn. It was her.

It had to be her....

Even though she was slim, her arms strained against the thin sleeves of her blouse as she lifted boxes into the back of the rusted SUV. She was running—just as he'd suspected she would.

Sebastian uttered a ragged sigh of frustration. While he was convinced she was the witness, he didn't know how to convince her to trust him. His promises of money and protection had only seemed to make her more leery and fearful of him.

Not that she didn't have reason to fear him. He could be the things she'd accused him of: ruthless, violent...

God, just looking through the scope brought back memories—horrible memories of hours spent watching and waiting for that perfect shot. The shot that terminated his target.

That sounded as impersonal and detached as he'd been, several hundred feet away from the life he'd taken. Was he taking hers now because he'd caused her to pack up and leave her home?

His military missions had had to be impersonal because he'd just been carrying out orders—orders that had served the greater good. Believing that was the only way he managed to sleep at night…when he actually managed to sleep.

The greater good was the very reason he was being so persistent now, why he couldn't leave her alone no matter how much she wanted him to. More was at stake than just her life—and her safety. All of them were in danger, including the child he believed she had but had yet to catch sight of…

Despite his years of training to control his physical reactions, his heart leaped—kicking against his ribs—as a nightmarish thought occurred to him. Was the child all right? Or was someone using him or her to keep the witness from sharing what she'd seen?

The woman swung the back door of the Suburban closed, then opened the driver's door and slid in behind the wheel. Alone. That booster chair in the backseat remained empty—hauntingly so.

"Where is your child, Mama?" Sebastian murmured as he jumped into his own vehicle.

He had parked on a little ridge a safe distance from

the ranch, out of her sight but so that she was within his. While he hadn't carried his sniper rifle—or his Kate, as the long-range Remington was sometimes called—in years, he occasionally carried the scope from it with him. That was the one thing he had liked about his years in the military, watching the world from a distance.

Before he pulled shut his driver's door, he noticed the starburst of sunlight refracting off another lens. He wasn't the only one watching from a distance. While he'd been watching the woman, someone else had been watching him from some scrubby trees on a hill in the badlands. Probably the men from the van…

He lifted his scope to point it toward the badlands where he'd noticed the starburst, but the window of the open driver's door exploded, shards of glass flying into the grass in which he'd parked. He reached for the door, but it shuddered as something hit again and embedded itself deep in the armrest inches from where his hand had been—where his heart might have been had he leaned farther out of the vehicle to use his scope.

Damn it! He was taking fire! His heart racing with adrenaline, he slammed the idling engine into Drive and tore down the ridge, putting it between him and the shooter. Taking away the shot…

Who the hell had been shooting at him? The men in the van? He was almost certain they'd had a gun. So had the woman, but she'd been back at the ranch, packing up her stuff. Could she have sent someone out to the badlands to fire at him and scare him off so she could get away?

No matter who'd shot at him, they would discover that Prince Sebastian Cavanaugh did not scare easily. He pressed harder on the accelerator so that the Hummer hurtled over the rough terrain, putting distance between him and the shooter and closing in on the distance between him and the woman. Dust swirled up from the dirt trail and through the broken driver's window, filling the Hummer like smoke.

He needed to call the sheriff and Antoine, and tell them he'd taken fire. But they would want him to head to the sheriff's office or the resort. And he was only going wherever the woman was going. She would not escape without telling him what she'd seen, without telling him where Amir was.

"Where the hell *are* you going?" he asked aloud, as she turned off the ranch drive and headed back toward town. Away from the badlands. If she'd sent the shooter there, she wasn't going to meet him.

Was she going to town to meet with the sheriff? Sebastian doubted that. It was more likely that she was off to meet with whoever might have her child. Maybe she'd sent her baby away to keep him safe and now she was off to join him.

And the baby's father?

Something twisted in his gut. It couldn't be jealousy. He had already determined that she was not his type, at least not the type of woman a prince was supposed to marry. She was beautiful. And vulnerable. And stubborn. And strong. But he wasn't attracted to her. He only felt responsible for her safety or current lack thereof.

So he followed her, at a safe distance that would make it hard for her to spot him but not to escape him. He had to be close. Close enough to come to her aid should she need it. And of course she did; she was just too stubborn to admit it and too scared to trust him.

"Where am I going?" a deep voice emanated from that damn speaker. "Why would you ask me such a question? I am here, at the resort. You are the one off on your own despite the fact that nearly anyone could have been bribed or bought to kill us."

He could not tell Antoine about the shooting. Not yet.

"Not everyone can be bought or bribed," Sebastian corrected his brother. He had tried both to get the woman to disclose what she'd seen. Perhaps he should have used intimidation.

"You have failed to bring the witness around?" Antoine surmised.

Just then the rusted SUV turned through the gates of the drive to Wind River Ranch and Resort. Was she coming to him?

"Perhaps I have not failed…" he murmured, more to himself than to his brother.

Relief flooded him that she was going to do the right thing. Because she had chosen to seek him out here at the resort, she had not sent a shooter after him, either.

Apparently she had not realized that he'd been up on that ridge. So someone else had been following him….

He shook his head, clearing those concerns from his mind. He would deal with that later. Now, with her here, he would finally learn what had happened to Amir.

But before he could turn into the resort behind her, another vehicle cut him off—careening into the drive ahead of him. A white van, like so many of the others filling the front parking lot of the resort—except for the crumpled driver's side.

It was definitely the one he had forced off the road. Whoever they were—and he was really starting to doubt it was reporters—they had found her again. And perhaps they had never lost him…

HER PULSE RACED as Jessica drove past the media vans parked at the grand entrance of the stone-and-cedar lodge. While security and sheriff's deputies kept the reporters, camera crews and picketing protestors out of the resort, they hovered around the entrance like vultures waiting for an injured animal to die.

For too long, Jessica had felt like that injured animal. But she was not going to helplessly wait for death.

She had to run…no matter how much leaving the ranch hurt her. Ducking her head low as she passed the vans and people, Jessica steered around the expansive building. With its impressive length and odd peaks and glittering windows, the lodge resembled a crown, so it was no mystery why the royals had chosen the luxurious resort for their summit meeting in the United States.

She maneuvered down the driveway that dropped off steeply at the side of the lodge to the back lot where the employees parked. There were no empty spots near the walkout basement side of the resort. There were barely any empty spots at all. The lot was full.

All the staff had been called in to work extra hours due to the royals extended stay. Despite the calluses and cracked skin on her hands, she could have used the extra hours because she could have definitely used the extra money.

But she hadn't wanted to be anywhere near this media frenzy—and those cameras that broadcast nationally. She didn't want to be here now. Nerves danced in her stomach and sweat trickled down between her shoulder blades, making her blouse stick to the vinyl seat. Even her palms grew damp, so much so that they slipped on the steering wheel as she pulled into a spot she made on the grass near the rear of the lot.

"I don't want to do this," she murmured, dread filling her at the thought of getting out of the SUV. It looked as though all the reporters waited at the front, but who was to say that one or two hadn't decided to stake out the back and interview the employees?

They had done that before, but Jessica had been careful to duck her head low so that they couldn't film her face. And she'd refused to answer any of their questions.

Maybe she should have asked Helen to retrieve her check instead of having her sit with Samantha. But what would it matter now if someone got a shot of her? By the time the footage aired, she and Samantha would be out of Wind River County. And they would never be able to return for fear that he might be here, waiting for them.

Urgency compelled her to throw open the door. The rusted hinges creaked in protest of the sudden movement, though. Or maybe in warning.

But she needed the money for gas and a place to stay until she could find another job. She doubted she would be lucky enough to find a friend as good as Helen again.

She blinked against the sting of tears at the thought of all she had to leave behind. Then she hurried toward the building, nearly jogging across the lot.

Tires squealed against asphalt, startling her into almost tripping and falling against the bumper of the white van that stopped in front of her. The driver's side was crumpled, but as she rounded the front, the sliding door on the passenger's side opened. And a burly man leaned out, his long arms reaching for her.

Earlier she'd wanted to draw no attention to her arrival at the resort. But now she opened her mouth and screamed, hoping someone would hear her and help her before it was too late.

SEBASTIAN'S BLOOD chilled as a scream pierced the warm air blowing through his driver's window. After the van had cut him off pulling into the resort, he'd lost it for a moment in the front lot when a car had backed up and blocked his pursuit. Just those few seconds of waiting for the car to get out of his way had given the men enough time to get to her.

He slammed the Hummer into Park behind the van but jumped out before it came to a complete stop. Its front bumper came to rest against the rear one of the already battered van.

More screams and grunts and curses rang out as two people struggled on the passenger's side of the van. One was a man, clad in suit pants and a button-down, striped shirt that wrinkled as his heavy muscles shifted beneath it. His dark hair was slicked back, probably with sweat as beads of it glistened on his furrowed forehead. He looked vaguely familiar, as if Sebastian had recently seen him.

Perhaps at the press conference…

But he obviously wasn't a reporter. He had to be one of the men hired to kill Sebastian and the other royals as well as the witness. Had he been the one who'd just fired at him?

The man struggled with the red-haired woman. She kicked, her legs swinging as the brute wrapped his arms around her, dragging her through the open sliding door into the cargo area of the van. But she put up a desperate fight, wriggling and clawing at him.

"Let me go!" she yelled.

"Let her go!" Sebastian shouted, echoing her order as he jumped into the fray.

The man did take one arm off her—to reach for his gun. Sebastian had his tucked into the small of his back. But could he risk the shot with the woman being used almost as a human shield, clutched tight in front of the man?

He had not fired a gun in years—too many years for him to trust his marksmanship was what it had once been. Legendary.

She reached out as far as she could with her arms pinned at her sides. Her hands extended toward Sebastian in supplication. Her dark eyes were wide, her gaze imploring him to provide the help he had promised her.

Sebastian could not fail to protect her. He would never be able to live with himself. At least when his father had failed his mother, the former bodyguard to the princess hadn't had to live with that failure.

But then Sebastian might not have to live with his failure, either. For the driver shouted something in what sounded like Russian. And then the man with the gun squeezed the trigger.

Chapter Six

Gunshots rang in Jessica's ears, momentarily deafening her. She flinched, but she couldn't close her eyes. Fear and horror gripped her too tightly, almost paralyzing her. Not only was she afraid for herself but also for the man who was trying to keep his word to her.

That he would protect her.

But he might die trying. The bullet had missed him, as if the man holding her hadn't really been trying to hit him. Just to scare him off. Apparently Prince Sebastian Cavanaugh didn't scare easily because he leaped forward, reaching for the man's gun. She couldn't tear her gaze from him as he grappled for it.

Why hadn't he tried to disarm her when she'd threatened him? He didn't seem at all concerned about this gun going off.

But it did, deafening Jessica again. She screamed, but she couldn't even hear her own voice—just a roaring in her ears. She focused on the prince, studying his handsome face for blood—or pain. Had he been hit?

If so, it wasn't enough to slow him down. He

reached for the man again, but before he could close his hands around the guy's wrist, the direction of the gun shifted.

"Back away!" the man yelled at the prince.

Cold metal pressed against Jessica's temple, chilling her skin. But she suppressed a shiver, afraid to move for fear that the gun would go off.

If it did, what would happen to her daughter? Would Helen keep her and raise her as her own? Or would the little girl's father track her down and claim custody? She couldn't die and leave her baby at the mercy of that monster.

"Back away," she implored her would-be protector, her gaze locked with his.

She had a feeling that this was a man who never backed away from any fight. But he lifted his hands and stepped back from the van.

"Don't hurt her," he ordered, but his words were more threat than command.

As if automatically obeying, the man shifted the gun away from her temple. Then he yelled at his partner behind the wheel, "Drive, damn it."

The van lurched back, into the vehicle the prince had been driving. Metal crunched against metal as tires and brakes burned. The impact threw her abductor off balance, and he fell to his side.

But the prince didn't move any farther away. As un-afraid as he'd been of the gun, he was also unafraid of getting caught in a crash. The van lurched forward now, striking a parked car and rocking it back into the one behind it.

Her abductor rolled toward the open door. If she didn't escape now, she might not have another chance. Shaking off the paralysis of fear, she struggled against the arm around her waist that locked her arms against her sides. She managed to wriggle out of his grasp and through the open sliding door of the still-moving vehicle.

She dropped onto her knees on the asphalt. The prince reached for her, to help her up. But the other man was there, his free hand tangling in her hair as he pointed the gun at the prince again. She kicked out and wriggled, but he dragged her back toward the van.

The earlier shots must have drawn attention from the resort because men were running across the parking lot. "Drive!" the man yelled again as he shoved her through the open door.

The prince grabbed the heavyset man, holding him back from jumping inside the van. Would the driver take off without him? The vehicle slammed into reverse, rubber squealing against the asphalt as it connected with the Hummer again with enough force to push it back a little.

As if he was afraid the driver would leave without him, the man attacked, slamming his gun against the prince's jaw. The prince staggered back but didn't fall. She rolled across the scratchy carpet and toward the open door. But the man was there, shoving her back as he jumped inside with her. He didn't come alone—the prince followed him, leaping into the van, too.

The man turned with his gun, directing it at Sebastian's handsome face. The van lurched as it squeezed between the vehicles it had been crashing into, knocking the heavyset man off balance.

Sebastian reached past him and locked his hand around Jessica's wrist. As the driver accelerated, the prince leaned back, falling out the door and tugging Jessica out with him. He landed with his back against the pavement, and Jessica cradled in his arms. Her breath rushed out of her lungs as the impact jarred her from head to toe.

She stared down into his face. His blue eyes were open and staring up into hers. But yet there was something about that almost-vacant stare that chilled her more than when the cold gun barrel had pressed against her temple.

"Are you all right?" Jessica asked as alarm gripped her—even as the van continued out of the parking lot.

Had his head struck the asphalt? Or had he been shot? As they'd fallen, she'd heard more gunfire—her ears rang with it as her heart raced with fear.

For his safety now.

"SEBASTIAN, WHAT THE HELL happened? Are you all right?"

His brother's deep voice roused him enough to break the connection with the beautiful woman he held as tightly as her would-be abductor had. Her soft body clasped against his, her breasts pushing into his chest, her hips thrust against his, her legs between his thighs.

He groaned, his body tensing in reaction to her closeness.

Tucking a gun into his suit jacket, Antoine asked, "Can you move?"

He could but didn't want to—not when it meant that she might move, too. She did anyway, shifting against him to glance toward his brother. Shock widened her eyes.

Ignoring his twin, Sebastian asked her, "Are you all right?"

Her gaze moved from his face to his brother's and back. "I—I think so."

"Your eyes are not deceiving you," Sebastian assured her. "This is my identical twin, Prince Antoine Cavanaugh." As occasionally happened, they had coincidentally dressed in similar dark suits and blue shirts.

"I believe we can forgo introductions right now," Antoine snapped. "Tell me what the hell happened."

Sebastian shook his head again. Maybe he had struck it, because he couldn't think clearly, not with the woman in his arms. Her hair felt like silk brushing across his jaw and her summer fresh scent filled his lungs as he drew in a deep breath. She smelled like flowers and rain-fresh breezes. He blew out a breath, trying to clear his head.

"Send a security team after that van," he said. He should have ordered that immediately, but his first concern had been *her*. Making certain she was all right. But he hadn't even been able to do that after landing so hard on the pavement.

"Already done," Antoine informed him, reaching down to offer him a hand up. "Brenner took off after it."

Sebastian didn't want to move yet. And not just because he wasn't convinced that he hadn't broken any bones. After almost losing her to the men in the van, he wanted to hang on to her awhile longer.

"As quickly as they were speeding away, I doubt they will be apprehended," Antoine warned him.

"Probably not," Sebastian agreed. He should have shot the man. He'd had the gun tucked into the waistband of his pants, where the barrel now scraped against his spine. But he hadn't wanted to risk her safety by putting her in the middle of flying bullets. But bullets had flown. Why hadn't the men tried harder to hit him?

The shots back on the ridge had been closer even though the distance had been greater. He furrowed his brow, trying to remember if he'd seen a long-range rifle in the back of the van. But he hadn't….

"Can you move?" Antoine asked after Sebastian had ignored his proffered hand.

"Not yet."

"You are hurt," she spoke again, quickly shifting her

slight weight off his body until she knelt beside him. Her small but strong hands skimmed down his sides, as if checking for injuries.

Too macho to admit the impact had knocked the wind out of him, he shook his head and sat up. "I'm fine."

Antoine grabbed his arm and helped him to his feet. "You're lucky you were not killed, brother."

His twin had his attention now, with the gruffness in his voice that couldn't quite hide his emotion. Sebastian could not imagine what Antoine had thought when he'd heard the shots and then found him lying on the ground. Actually, regrettably, he could imagine because they shared some gruesome memories.

"I am fine," he assured his brother again. He would tell him about the earlier shots—later.

Antoine stared at him for a moment before nodding in acceptance of his claim.

Sebastian turned to the woman, reaching for her arms to help her up. She flinched but perhaps in pain and not just fear this time. "Are you really all right?" he asked her.

"Perhaps I should have not forestalled the introductions," Antoine murmured. "Who is she, brother? The witness?"

It was about damn time Sebastian found out for certain. So he swung her up in his arms and headed toward the resort, shoving past the reporters and security personnel that the gunfire had drawn to the scene. Instead of fighting him, the woman turned her face and buried it against his neck, her breath warming his skin and his blood.

FOR THE SECOND TIME in years, a man held Jessica in his arms. But his grasp was neither painful nor so tight that she probably wouldn't have been able to struggle free. But yet he was still threatening, even after he had risked his life for hers.

Or had he only risked his life to learn what she'd seen that night. Either way, he had saved her from the men and the throng of reporters gathered outside the resort.

"You will not lie to me again," he warned her as he kicked a door closed behind them, locking her inside one of the luxurious suites in the resort. Alone with him. He loosened his grasp, dropping the arm from beneath her legs, so that she slid down his muscular body.

Her skin heated and tingled at the sensation. She lifted her palms to his chest—and pushed—so that there was finally some space between them. But still she couldn't breathe, her lungs full and aching as his gaze held her as tightly as his arms had.

"You will tell me the truth about that night," he demanded, as he continued to stare at her. Even with his golden brown hair tousled and his dark suit wrinkled and torn, he looked regal. Imperious.

And to him, she—in her worn and ragged clothing—must look like a vagrant. In a short while, she and Samantha would be homeless. Unless she told him what he wanted to know and accepted his reward. She needed the money, but she couldn't take it. But could she tell him what he wanted to know? Didn't she owe him after he'd saved her?

"What did you see?" Prince Sebastian asked.

Stalling for time, she replied, "You keep assuming that I'm the witness."

"I'm not the only one making such an assumption," he pointed out. "Those men who tried to abduct you also believe you are the witness."

After what she'd heard in the van, she doubted those men worked for whoever was trying to kill the royals. No, she suspected that they worked for someone far more dangerous—at least to her.

DMITRI HELD THE PHONE away from his ear as Russian curses burst from it. When they wound down, he lifted it to his face again.

"I am sorry," he apologized. "The prince is tougher than you figured."

"Or maybe you are just much weaker than I figured," the boss replied.

Pride and most of his muscles stinging, Dmitri almost uttered a curse of his own, but he bit it back. It didn't matter how far away the boss was, there were conse-quences to getting him mad. Painful consequences. "Prince Sebastian keeps getting in the way."

"This will be the last time he gets in the way."

"You want us to kill him?" Dmitri asked, eagerness easing the sting of his pride. He had wanted to in the parking lot; he had actually fired at him a couple of times. But the prince's reflexes were quick. And no matter what the boss believed, the royal was strong.

"You proceed with the next part of the plan," the boss ordered. "I will personally take care of Prince Sebastian Cavanaugh."

"You are here?" Dmitri asked, glancing outside the van. The driver had parked in the middle of nowhere—far from the road where sirens wailed as police cars approached the resort.

"I will be soon. And when I get there, Prince Sebastian will no longer be in the way. He will be dead."

Dmitri clicked off the phone and shuddered. The boss did not make idle threats. Prince Sebastian Cavanaugh was already as good as dead.

Chapter Seven

"What are you so afraid of?" Sebastian asked, hating the fear that had drained the color from her face and left her eyes so wide and so very dark.

She tilted her head and stared up at him, incredulous. "After what just happened, how can you ask me that?" She trembled. "Those men—"

"Would have you in that van now if not for me." Rage heated his blood at the thought of her in that burly man's grasp. She so delicate and fragile and the man so brutish and strong.

Her breath escaped in a shaky gasp. "You are so arrogant."

He shrugged. "I need to have some arrogance or I would not be able to lead my country." Or he would let that voice in his head, the one that told him he wasn't good enough, undermine his confidence.

Her lips curved into a slight smile. "You would consider that an attribute instead of a flaw."

"It is an attribute," he said. "Like integrity and trustworthiness, which I also possess."

Her smile widened, brightening her pale face. "Of course."

No doubt he sounded pompous, but that was not his intent. "I am trying to convince you that you can trust me."

Her smile faded. "I can't trust anyone."

The certainty in her voice clenched his heart. "You can trust *me*," he insisted. "Did I not protect you as I promised I would?"

"Yes. Yes." She nodded. "And I owe you my gratitude for stepping in and risking your life like you did."

"You owe me the truth," he said. "Admit that you witnessed the explosion."

She shook her head and turned toward the door he'd kicked closed moments ago.

Sebastian could physically stop her and probably would before he let her open that door and just walk out. But he tried one more time to get through to her rationally. "At least have the decency to tell me if my friend is alive or dead."

She stilled, her body tense.

He held his breath, waiting for her to refuse him again. Then perhaps he would need to turn her over to Antoine. His brother could make her talk; he could make anyone talk. But Sebastian didn't want her hurt or frightened or manipulated. He suspected she'd already been in that position too many times.

"Alive," she replied in a tremulous whisper. "The last time I saw him, he was alive."

His breath shuddered out in a sigh of pure relief. "He's alive?"

"He was…right after the explosion. But I think he was hurt."

Some of his relief fled as concern rushed back. They had already known he was hurt, though, because forensics expert, Jane Cameron, had admitted they'd found Amir's blood in the limo. A lot of blood.

"Didn't you help him?"

She shook her head. "I was a distance behind the limo when it exploded. It looked as though he must have been thrown clear."

Perhaps Amir hadn't been hurt that badly then. But if he hadn't, why hadn't he returned to the resort or at least contacted one of them?

"You didn't get closer to the scene?" he asked, wondering if her tire tracks had been the ones that Jane had found at the site of the explosion. Jane could check out the rusted Suburban now.

As Sebastian had carried this woman away from the parking lot, the other royals had been rushing toward it. Prince Stefan Lutece would call Jane, if she wasn't already at the resort. Since meeting after the explosion, the two had rarely been apart. Sebastian would need to speak with Jane later about pulling the bullet from the armrest of his door.

"I got closer," the woman said with a shudder. "I saw the driver." Her delicate features twisted into a grimace at the memory of what she'd seen. "It was too late to help him."

"I know." He stepped up behind her and closed his hands over her slender shoulders.

She shuddered again.

"I am sorry you had to see that." It was never easy seeing someone die, not even through a scope at long distance.

"That was when I left the scene," she said.

He tightened his grasp on her shoulders and spun her around to face him. "Without waiting to see if Amir was all right?"

"By the time I had driven up closer to the burning limo, he was already gone."

"Gone? How? If he was injured, he couldn't have outrun your vehicle."

"Someone picked him up," she said. "With all the flames and the smoke, I wasn't able to see who. From the height of the taillights as it drove off, I figure it was some kind of truck or SUV. But most people drive trucks or SUVs around here."

His relief was short-lived as his concern turned to dread. "So anyone could have driven off with him. Even a white van?"

She nodded. "I'm sorry. It could have been."

And if it had been, it was no wonder that Amir had not contacted them. Even though the explosion hadn't killed him, those men would have, had they gotten hold of the sheik. And no doubt if Sebastian hadn't gotten her away from them, they would have killed her, too.

JESSICA'S HEAD POUNDED and her throat had grown raspy from all the questions she'd answered. Not for Sebastian. She'd told him what he'd wanted to hear, but then he had called the others into the room. And she'd had to repeat her story to the other royals, to the forensics expert, Jane Cameron, and to Sheriff Wolf. They had all taken turns interrogating her, and his twin had studied her as she'd replied, as if he were a human lie detector.

She had no idea if she'd passed or failed. All the others had left the room except for the man identical to the one who'd saved her. She suspected his twin did not approve of the risk Prince Sebastian had taken to protect her. Although they talked in low tones, their deep voices vibrated with anger, as if they were arguing.

Over her?

Finally Prince Antoine stepped into the hall, and Sebastian nearly slammed the door between them because he shut it with such force.

"I'm sorry," she murmured.

"Why? You told the truth, right?" he asked, fixing her with that implacable stare.

She nodded. "Of course."

He crossed the sitting area to the desk and pulled open a drawer. He took out a pen and a checkbook, scribbled out something and then tore the check free of the book. He walked back to her and held it out between them.

She clasped her hands together, unwilling to reach for it.

"Take it," he ordered, pressing the check into her hand.

Her fingers trembled, rustling the piece of paper. Then she noticed the amount and dropped the check as shock filled her. "I—I can't."

He bent over to pick it up, and a grimace contorted his handsome face.

"You're hurt," she said, and reached out in concern, her hands sliding under his shoulders to help him back up. He'd discarded his suit jacket and wore only a silk dress shirt in a blue nearly as deep as his eyes. Her palms skimmed over the expensive fabric and the hard muscles that rippled beneath it. "You should have a doctor check you out."

"I don't need a doctor," the prince said, his body so tense as he stood close to her that she felt the deep breath he dragged into his lungs. "I just need the whole truth from you."

"I told you everything I saw that night, which wasn't much. That's why I can't take your money." She couldn't take a reward for doing the right thing. While she'd had her doubts earlier about telling him that the missing sheik survived the explosion, she believed that Prince

Sebastian was a true friend to the man. He would not cause him any harm.

Jessica wasn't sure that he wouldn't cause her any harm, though. Just touching him had her heart racing at an almost painful pace. She jerked her hands off him and stepped back.

But Prince Sebastian followed her, standing so close that his legs brushed against her thighs. His chest and abdomen also rubbed against her breasts. Awareness pooled low in her stomach, spreading heat from the tips of her breasts to the very core of her.

"Is that the only reason you won't take my check?" he asked.

"Yes."

"You don't have another reason?"

"Pride? I can't afford to be proud," she admitted although she probably didn't need to point that out to him. He had to see how she dressed, what she drove.

"Then why won't you take this?" He held up the check. "Because you can't cash it?"

"I won't cash it." She stepped back again and turned toward the door. "So keep it."

He caught her wrist and spun her around to face him. "Is Jessica Peters your real name?"

"Wh-why would you ask me that?"

"Because my brother says you're lying about your name, that you're hiding your real identity."

God, the man really was a human lie detector.

"I will deny it if you tell him this, but my brother is rarely wrong."

She couldn't help but smile at his admission of sibling rivalry. But then a pang of loss clutched at her heart. She'd had a brother, too, and had been as close as the royal twins, if not closer. Because their single mom hadn't been the most reliable guardian, Sam had been as much parent as brother to her. Hell, Sam had been everything to her. And when he'd died, she'd lost everything, even her common sense.

But now she had her daughter whom she'd named after her brother. She couldn't lose Samantha, too, and that could happen if anyone discovered her real identity. She drew in a shaky breath and asked, "So you think I'm lying about my name, too?"

"I think you changed your name." He caught a lock of her hair between his fingers. "I think you tried to change how you look."

His brother wasn't the only observant Cavanaugh. She held her lips closed, unwilling to say any more. She'd agreed to tell him what she'd witnessed but nothing else.

"I thought you had dyed your hair to hide from the people seeking the witness," he continued. "But I have a feeling you've been hiding from someone else and for much longer than two weeks."

She shivered at his insightfulness—and at the horrible memories that rushed over her.

"Who are you hiding from, Jessica, or whatever your real name is?"

"I'm Jessica," she said, then relented. "Now." She didn't want to hear her old name ever again. She didn't want to go back to that old life, not even in memories. But as she'd already learned, the prince was relentless when he wanted to know something. No doubt he would keep at her until she told him what he wanted to know—what she'd never wanted to talk about again.

"Who are you hiding from?"

"My husband."

SEBASTIAN FELT AS THOUGH he had struck the pavement again. She was married. When he'd seen the car seat, he'd realized she was a mother and had even considered that she might be a wife.

But having confirmation…

"Why are you hiding from your husband?" he had to know.

"Because he told me that if I ever left him, he would track me down and kill me." She said it matter-of-factly—fatalistically—as if she had every reason to believe her husband would follow through on the threat he had made.

"He was abusive." That explained the reason she'd flinched whenever Sebastian had reached out to touch her.

"Yes." Color rushed to her face. "But I—I didn't know

that about him…until after we were married. And then it was too late."

"Had you tried to leave him before?"

"Yes," she said, "when he was in prison."

He wanted to ask her what the man had done that had sent him away. But her story was difficult for her to share; he didn't want to make it any more traumatic for her.

"He was serving seven years on an assault charge," she offered, surprising him.

When he gasped, she added, "Not me. He'd lost his temper with someone who worked with him—put the man in a coma. Of course he told me it was self-defense, that the man had assaulted him first."

"You believed him?"

"No, but no one calls Evgeny Surinka a liar. I was relieved when he went to prison. But he had people watching me," she continued, "making sure I didn't leave."

"You had no one to help you escape him?" Had she been all alone?

"My brother died before I married Evgeny. He was all I had."

Until now. Now she had him—if she would accept his offer of protection. "So you stayed?"

"I tried to leave," she said. "I filed for divorce while he was in prison."

"What happened?"

A soft cry escaped her lips. "He got out."

"Jessica…"

"That was almost five years ago."

"He hurt you."

She flinched as if reliving the pain. "That first night he got out, he put me in the hospital."

"Oh, my God…"

Her breath shuddered out, as if with relief. "But that's how I got away. A nurse realized what had happened and who he was. She gave me some money and a bus ticket. She helped me leave."

"Where did you leave?"

"New York."

Not only had she changed her appearance but also her speech. He detected no trace of city in her soft voice. "You put a lot of distance between the two of you. No wonder he hasn't found you."

"Until now," she said, the color draining from her face again to leave her eyes so dark and haunted.

"He was one of those men in the van?" If so, Sebastian wished to hell that he'd taken the damn shot now.

"No." She shuddered. "But they are his men."

"He has men? Who is he?"

"Evgeny Surinka," she repeated the man's name. But it meant nothing to Sebastian. She added, "He emigrated to the United States with his father when he was just a twelve-year-old kid. His father is an infamous Russian mobster. Or he was, until Evgeny took over."

No wonder she had been hiding for so many years. To protect herself and her child.

"And do you have a child?" he asked.

"A daughter." A smile lit up her face so that it glowed with love. Her beauty stole away his breath for a moment. "She's four."

"Where is she? Is someone holding her?"

"She's safe at the ranch with my friend Helen Jeffries. Helen owns the Double J. She would never let anyone take Samantha. She treats her like she's her granddaughter. Hell, Samantha might be safer with Helen than she is with me. Evgeny doesn't know about her," she said. Her voice cracking with emotion and old pain, she added, "I didn't know I was pregnant when I left."

During his years as a military sniper, Sebastian had had to kill marks he'd never met—because it had been ordered. This was the first time he wanted to give the order for the kill, the first time that he wanted to pull the trigger out of vengeance rather than duty. No matter, though, killing Evgeny Surinka would definitely be for the greater good.

"He can never find out about Samantha," Jessica said, her voice breaking with fear and sobs. "He would hurt her to hurt me."

Sebastian pulled her into his arms, clasping her trembling body close. "He won't hurt either of you. I won't let him."

"You won't be able to stop him. No one can stop him," she said, her voice rising with hysteria. "I just need to get away. I need to go back to the ranch, get Samantha and run as far as I can, like I did last time."

"You don't know that he has found you," he said. "Some of the hit men hired to kill us have connections to the Russian mob." He drew in a breath and admitted what he'd just shared with Antoine. "I was shot at earlier today. I was alone. It had nothing to do with you."

He believed that now. There was no way this woman would have asked someone to shoot at him—even just to scare him off. She'd already had more than enough violence in her life. So had he, really.

"You were shot at earlier? Are you okay?" she asked, her dark eyes brimming with concern.

He nodded. "They missed."

"Who shot at you? The men from the van?"

"I don't know. I couldn't see who it was." That was all he'd been able to tell his brother, too, much to his disgruntlement. But Antoine was going to have Jane take the bullet from the Hummer and run ballistics on it. He'd wanted Sebastian to show Jane where the shooting had happened as well, but he could not leave Jessica alone.

"Then it could have been someone else who shot at you, whoever blew up that limo. But I know who's after me. Evgeny."

"A hit was put out on you, too," he warned her. "Because of what you witnessed. That has nothing to do with your ex."

She stared up at him hopefully, as if wanting to believe him, but tears of fear and horror filled her dark eyes. She would rather a hired assassin be after her than her husband. "I can't take that chance," she said. "I have to leave Wind River. Now."

"Not now," he said, tightening his arms around her. He couldn't let her go and not just because he was worried about her safety.

He just couldn't let her go. He lowered his head and pressed his mouth to hers.

Chapter Eight

Jessica's lips parted on a gasp of surprise. A prince was kissing her?

Was she dreaming? Perhaps it was all a dream, and she was standing at the sink, her hands in soapy water while she watched his press conference and fantasized about him. But she was no Cinderella.

And this was no dream.

His lips were warm and real and surprisingly silky given the hard look of his mouth and the firmness of his jaw. He deepened the kiss, slipping his tongue through her open lips.

He tasted as he smelled—rich and regal. While she was no Cinderella, he was definitely a prince—from the inside out. But his arrogance was earned and maybe, as he'd claimed, necessary even to lead.

She'd bristled at following his earlier orders, but now she willingly followed where he led her. She kissed him back, sliding her tongue over his. Pushing her fingers into his thick, soft hair, she pulled him closer as she stretched up his hard body, her arms wrapped around his neck.

He kissed her passionately but gently. His mouth was greedy but not cruel. His hands moved over her, sliding up and down her back, grasping her hips, but his touch was a sensual caress.

She had never known such tenderness and couldn't believe that a man who'd fought as hard as he had to protect her was capable of such tenderness. Maybe it was gratitude over his saving her that drew her to him. Maybe it was the adrenaline from that dangerous experience that had her blood pumping so fast and hot in her veins that had her trembling with desire.

He must have mistaken her reaction for fear because he pulled back and soothed her. "Jessica, it's all right. I would never hurt you."

She wanted to believe him. But mostly she just wanted him. So she tugged his head back down to hers, initiating the kiss this time as she moved her mouth over his.

He groaned against her lips. Then his arms wound around her again, lifting her from the floor so that her breasts pressed into his hard chest and her hips thrust against his. He was hard and ready for her, his erection straining the fly of his dress pants. She arched and rubbed, aching for his possession, as pressure built inside her.

He walked backward through an open door in the suite. Passing through it, they entered the bedroom. The sheets had already been turned down, inviting him to lay her upon the cool satin. Then he followed her down, pressing her into the downy soft mattress.

Jessica had occasionally made these beds, when she'd filled in for housekeeping, but she had never lain in one. And she shouldn't be doing so now. She tensed beneath him, but he kept kissing her, his hands reaching between them, skimming over her breasts to the mismatched buttons of her blouse.

Would he stop if she asked? Or was he so used to getting what he wanted that he would just take her?

But why would Sebastian want her? She was the battered wife of a Russian mobster, and he was a prince. They had no future together even if Evgeny wasn't determined to kill her.

WHEN SEBASTIAN REALIZED that she had gone still beneath him, he struggled for control. Gasping for breath, he rolled away from her and sat up on the edge of the bed.

"I'm sorry," he apologized, horrified at his own behavior. He never lost control as he just had with her. "I had no right to take such liberties."

She'd already thought him arrogant. What must she think now? That he was as ruthless and violent as her husband?

"I apologize for taking advantage of you," he continued.

"You didn't take advantage," she said.

"You have been through too much today to think clearly."

"You're not thinking clearly, either," she said, absolving him of complicity. "Or you would want nothing to do with me, Prince Sebastian."

"Sebastian," he automatically corrected her. He did not want her using anything but his first name. Not Prince. Not Your Highness or Your Majesty—nothing that reminded him that he was royalty, and according to his grandfather, had an obligation to marry only royalty.

"Sebastian…" she repeated his name quietly as her face flushed with embarrassment.

"You filed for divorce years ago," he said, assuring her that they had not done anything immoral. Not even close. It had been just a kiss, or that was what he desperately wanted to believe. But he had never reacted so strongly to just a kiss—not even from those beautiful princesses and heiresses he'd dated in the past.

Perhaps that was why he'd never married one, no matter that he and his brother needed heirs to protect the future of Barajas nearly as much as they needed the trade agreement with the United States.

"I'm sure Evgeny contested the divorce, though, and it didn't go through," she said.

"But you've been separated for years." Because she had run away and hidden from the monster.

"It doesn't matter," Jessica said, her voice bleak and

her expressive eyes eerily blank. "Evgeny will never let me go."

"Because you won't let him," Sebastian replied, hoping to bring back her indomitable spirit.

"What do you mean?" she asked defensively. "I've been hiding from him for years."

"Yes, but he's still here." He reached out and tapped her temple. "In your head. You've never escaped him. You carry him with you."

"I couldn't forget him," she admitted. "I couldn't let my guard down, either, because I always knew that he would find me again. And now he has."

"You don't know that," Sebastian said. "You're jumping to conclusions."

"No." She shook her head. "I am convinced that those men are working for Evgeny."

"Why? Because they spoke Russian? As I told you, one of the hit men was Russian. It is a coincidence—a horrible coincidence—that is all." Jessica wasn't the only one with Russian mob connections. One of the island nations that neighbored Barajas that had refused to participate in COIN had mob connections.

She shook her head again, swirling her hair around her shoulders. "No."

"It is a more likely coincidence than Evgeny finding you just after you've witnessed an explosion."

"I always knew he would find me someday."

"How could you be so certain that he would, given how well you've hidden from him?" She was not giving herself enough credit. Not only had she escaped her abusive husband but she'd also eluded him for years.

"I knew he would find me because I knew that he would never stop looking until he did."

"But you don't know that he has found you," Sebastian insisted. "I think it is more likely that those men are working for whoever is behind the explosion that nearly claimed Amir's life."

She reached out now and squeezed his hand. "The explosion did not kill him," she assured him. "He was alive."

Was. He had no assurances that Amir still was, and she could offer him none. But he could offer her assurances—if only she would put aside her fear and listen to him. And trust him. But how could she trust him when he'd nearly forced himself on her?

Especially after what she'd confided in him about Evgeny's abuse.

He entwined his fingers with hers, surprised again at the calluses and strength of her small hand. "Thank you."

"For what?" she asked. "I should have come forward right after the explosion."

"You were afraid that the press might catch you on camera." As they probably had at the sheriff's office. "And Evgeny might see you on the news."

"Yes," she admitted. "But I also believed that your friend might be safer if no one knew he was alive."

"You didn't know who to trust."

"Do you?" she asked.

Sebastian sighed. "Some of our own men have betrayed us," he admitted. "And there is corruption in the police department and sheriff's office."

"So you understand why I was afraid to come forward?"

"I understand."

"Then you must understand why I have to leave, too. I need to get back to the ranch, finish packing and leave Wind River County."

"You don't have to leave," he said. "I can help you."

Her chin snapped up with her pride. "I don't want your money."

"Then take my protection," he urged her.

"I just told you that I don't know who to trust."

"You can trust me. I will protect you."

She leaned forward and brushed her lips across his. "Don't make promises you can't keep."

It was as if she knew, as if she, too, could hear that voice inside his head, the one that taunted him—convincing him that he was just like his father. That he, too, would fail to protect those who mattered most to him.

Jessica didn't matter most to him. But given that he'd just met her, she mattered more than she should.

Too much for him to lose…

WHILE SHE HAD REFUSED to accept his money and his protection, she had accepted Sebastian's escort back to the ranch. But she couldn't glance toward the driver's seat without heat rushing to her face. Her whole body burned, her skin tingling everywhere he had touched her.

Why had she let him touch her? He was practically a stranger to her. She knew nothing about him except what she'd learned from the media. But the reporters hadn't told her how rich and seductive he tasted, or how hard and muscular his long body was.

She had learned that for herself. And now she wished she could unlearn it—that she could just forget they had ever kissed. She also wished she could pretend that they might not have done more if she hadn't remembered who they were.

He was a prince. But he didn't look particularly regal now. He'd changed from his crumpled dark suit into jeans and a plaid shirt with the sleeves rolled to his elbows. Behind the wheel of the rusted Suburban, he looked more ranch hand than royal. If he'd covered his golden brown hair with a Stetson or Resistol, he could have passed for a cowboy.

But it was just a disguise, like her red dye and straightened hair—something so that he could slip past the press surrounding the resort. After the police had been called to the scene of the near-abduction, the media had grown more frenzied—like sharks sensing blood in the water.

"You didn't need to drive me back to the ranch," she said. Again.

Just like the first few times she'd told him that, he ignored her and continued to drive, his hands grasping the wheel tightly. His jaw taut, he stared straight ahead.

"I told you everything I know about the explosion." She was only sorry it wasn't more. "Shouldn't you be using that information to find your friend?"

"We have already been searching for him," Sebastian said.

"Even before you knew if he was still alive?"

"He is our friend," he replied, as if loyalty was a matter of fact. "We will not rest until we find out what happened to him and where he is."

Like Evgeny would not rest until he found her. Their motives were different but their eerily similar determination unsettled her. She shivered.

"You are cold?" He rolled up the window, shutting out the warm breeze.

A chill raised goose bumps on her skin, but it had nothing to do with the temperature and everything to do with Evgeny. While the prince wanted her to trust him, he didn't trust her. He didn't believe her claim that Evgeny had found her.

"I'm fine." Or she would be once she had Samantha with her and they were as far from Wind River County as they could get. "You really don't need to be concerned about me. I can take care of myself." She had been doing so for years.

"You tell me that you believe your abusive ex has

found you and that he intends to kill you and you think I can just walk away?"

"Other men would run," she replied, knowing so many who hadn't wanted to get involved with her because Evgeny had made it clear she was his and his alone. Even when he'd been in prison, she'd had no life because his or his father's men had watched her and scared off her friends and anyone who might have wanted to become more than friends.

"I am not other men," he said with the arrogance that made her smile now. "I am a prince."

"And I am not one of your subjects," she reminded him. "You are not *my* prince." No matter how much she might fantasize that he could have been. "You are not responsible for me or my safety."

He turned off to the ranch, driving past the sign for the Double J, or as it appeared, T. "If these men are, as I believe, after you because of what you witnessed, then you are most definitely my responsibility. After you spoke to the others, word could have leaked out that revealed your identity."

"But I didn't really see anything, not anything that will lead back to who planted the bomb or even tell you where the sheik is."

"But everyone might not believe you shared everything that you witnessed."

"Do you?"

Pulling up near the house, he braked the Suburban and turned toward her. He studied her with that implacable stare of his before replying, "I do."

She expelled a shaky breath of relief. She didn't want him to think that she'd held anything back that could help him find his friend or the people after them. "Thank you…"

"For believing you?"

"And for the ride. But how will you get back to the resort?" She couldn't drive him back. She and Samantha needed to leave the ranch right away.

"I will drive back…with you and your daughter. I want to make sure that the two of you will be safe. So I will not let you out of my sight."

She shivered again as his words echoed those another man had vowed to her. She had eventually escaped Evgeny, though.

Could she escape the prince? Did she want to?

His body tensed, his hands gripping the wheel as his stare went beyond her to the front door. She turned to follow his gaze and her heart slammed against her ribs. The door was open, the jamb splintered.

"Oh, my God!" Her hands shaking, she threw open the passenger's door, jumped down from the SUV and ran toward the steps to the porch. "Samantha! Helen!"

She had thought that because Evgeny didn't know about his daughter that the child would be safe—safer even when her mother wasn't around. But she'd been wrong. Evgeny hadn't just come back for her. He'd come back for their child, too.

Was she too late to stop him from taking what mattered even more to her than her own life?

Chapter Nine

Sebastian caught Jessica just as she was running up the steps to the porch. He wrapped one arm around her waist and clasped his palm across her mouth. "Shh… they could still be inside."

Her eyes widened, her fear edging toward hysteria.

"I'll go in first," he said. "You call Sheriff Wolf." He pressed his cell into her hand and gently pushed her back toward the Suburban.

She hesitated and opened her mouth, as if about to argue with him. Then he withdrew his gun from the waistband of his jeans. She nodded and, with shaking fingers, punched numbers into his phone.

Forcing his heart rate to steady and his breathing to slow and even out, he crept up onto the porch, the worn stair treads barely creaking beneath his weight. Even before his military training, he'd learned how to move without making a sound. His gun drawn, he stepped through the open door into the foyer. Buckshot had torn the faded wallpaper on the foyer walls and peppered the door with holes, so that sunlight shone through it like Swiss cheese.

Something horrible had happened here. Sebastian blamed himself. That van must have followed him earlier despite his efforts to run them off. And when Sebastian had thwarted their attempt at the resort to grab Jessica, they had come back to the ranch to wait for her. Or perhaps it had been the other shooter—the one from the badlands—who had been watching him all along.

Jessica's friend, the owner of the ranch, must have tried to stop them. Where were they—the woman and the little girl?

He had not seen the van or any other vehicle, so he was almost certain the people who'd broken into the house were gone. Otherwise he would not have left Jessica alone outside. But still, he moved silently through the house, in case one of them had stayed behind. He peered through archways into rooms filled with overturned furniture.

A moan emanated from behind a closed door. He carefully pushed it open, as far as he was able with a body lying behind it.

Blood. So much blood…it flashed him back to other bodies he'd found. But that had been a long time ago, so he shook off the old memories.

He dropped to his knees to check for a pulse. But before he could reach out, floorboards creaked behind him. There was someone else in the house. He ducked behind the door and lifted his gun. Although he had not fired one since his last deployment, he was ready to shoot.

And kill.

THE PRINCE'S PHONE clutched in her hand like a weapon, Jessica ventured into the only real home she and her daughter had ever known. Seeing the bullet holes and damage to that home had her flinching with pain. She fought down the scream and the sobs that burned her throat.

She couldn't give in to panic now, not when her daughter and Helen needed her. And maybe Sebastian needed her, too. While she'd waited—those agonizingly long minutes outside—she hadn't heard anything. Not a gunshot. Not a shout. Not even a cry for help.

What had happened? Where was everyone?

A murmur emanated from the phone, but she pressed her hand tighter over it. She didn't want to give away her presence in the house. But she also didn't want to break her connection with the sheriff's office, either. They were on their way, but they'd wanted her to stay on the phone and keep them apprised of the situation.

She had no damn idea what the situation was. Or where her friend and her daughter were. Shaking with fear, she crept down the hall. She glanced through the archways into the front parlor and the living room as she passed them. The rooms were empty but for overturned furniture and pulled-out drawers.

She crossed the wide hall to the dining room and

pushed open the door…as far as it would go against the body blocking it. Before she could look down to see who was lying on the floor, something else caught her attention.

The barrel of the gun pointed directly at her face. She sucked in a breath, but before she could expel it in a scream, the gun lowered. And the prince stepped out from behind the door.

"Damn it, Jessica," Sebastian said, his voice low with frustration. "I told you to wait outside. I have not yet secured the house." But instead of rushing off to another room, he dropped to his knees beside the body.

And so did Jessica, her heart rising to her throat and choking her as she saw all the blood. It stained her friend's gray hair and covered her swollen face. "Helen!"

"She's alive," Sebastian assured her, his fingers closed around the older woman's wrist. "But she needs an ambulance."

Jessica thrust the phone at him. "They're sending out police cars." She hadn't asked for an ambulance. She'd hoped they wouldn't need one. Tears streamed down her face as she leaned over her friend.

Was the woman even conscious?

The prince spoke into the phone, giving them his assessment of Helen's injuries and relaying the urgency for medical assistance.

"Helen, I'm so sorry," she murmured. "So sorry…"

The ranch owner moaned and shifted on the floor.

Jessica reached for her hand. Helen's nails were torn; she'd fought off her attackers. "Helen, where is Samantha? Did he get her?"

The older woman tried to squeeze Jessica's hand, but her grip was weak and her hand dropped back to the floor. If Helen had been conscious when they'd found her, she wasn't now.

"Helen!"

"She's breathing. An ambulance is coming. She'll be all right," the prince assured her. His arm slid around her shoulders, offering comfort as well as protection. He kept glancing around, checking the corners of the room for Helen's attackers.

"Stay with her," he said, "while I check the rest of the house."

Removing his arm and his protection, he left the room then. He left her alone at Helen's side, clutching the battered woman's limp hand. Jessica wasn't worried about him coming across the men who had so horribly beaten her friend.

But for them, the house felt empty. Too quiet now that Helen had stopped moaning, so that no one else could have still been inside. She didn't even hear Sebastian moving around; he moved more silently than the wind that blew through an open window. She only noticed his return because she felt his presence.

"They're gone," he said, his hand dropping to her shoulder and squeezing gently as he leaned over her.

"What about Samantha?" she asked, the words

burning her heart as well as her throat. If the child had been hiding, she would have come out when she'd heard Jessica's voice. "Where is my little girl?"

HER VOICE, THICK with emotion as she asked that heartbreaking question, reached inside Sebastian and squeezed his heart in a tight fist.

"We'll find her," he promised and hoped it was a promise he would be able to keep. "The police will be here soon, as will Antoine and the most trusted members of our security detail. We will begin an extensive search for her then."

She squeezed her friend's hand and then lurched to her feet. "If she's not already gone, she'll be hiding. I taught her to hide if strangers ever tried to break into the ranch."

Darkness filled Sebastian's mind, blinding him to all but the past. Memories pummeled him, memories of hiding in the dark, of daring not to breathe, of trying to quiet even his own heartbeat so that they were not discovered. But unlike the child who might be hiding alone, he'd had Antoine. He'd had chubby fingers clutching his hand, reminding him that he was not alone.

He cleared the emotion of those old memories from his throat and asked, "Where would she hide?"

Jessica glanced to the open window. "She could be anywhere. I taught her to run and hide."

Many years ago, his father had taught him and Antoine that same serious game of hide and hope like hell to never be found.

Sirens wailed, announcing the arrival of the police cars and the ambulance. But beneath that noise, Sebastian heard another one. A faint clunk of something dropping and rolling across a hardwood floor.

He reached for his gun again, but Jessica clutched his hand and stopped him.

"Maybe it's her," she said, hope lifting her voice. "Maybe she's still here."

Or perhaps one of the men had been left behind and Sebastian hadn't discovered him in his first search of the house. Before he could share that concern with Jessica, she rushed off to follow the noise coming from the back of the house, under the stairwell that led up from the country kitchen to the second story. The empty space beneath the steps had been enclosed with oak cabinets and doors to add to the cupboard space of the kitchen.

When Jessica reached for the handle on the pantry door, he caught her wrist and stopped her. "You don't know that it's her."

"No man would fit in there," she said. "The space is too shallow." She shrugged off his grasp and pulled open the door.

A broom, a bucket and a vacuum cleaner filled the space. There was no small body cowering inside.

He squeezed Jessica's shoulder, knowing that she must be filled with disappointment. But she reached inside the pantry and pushed aside the back panel of the cupboard to reveal another dark space, one that led deeper under the stairs and had no light except for the flashlight that rolled across the floor. But it was turned off or burned out.

The unlit hiding space brought him back more than thirty years to that dark closet in which he and Antoine had hidden. They hadn't been able to see anything... until much later when they had finally crawled out.

But they'd heard everything. And they'd felt everything.

"Samantha!" Jessica called out, fear cracking her voice. "Baby, are you in there?"

And if the child was hiding in the dark space, she would be able to hear and feel how terrified her mother was. The terror radiated off Jessica in waves that were drowning her and probably threatened to tow the child under with her.

Because the four-year-old could feel Jessica's fear, he was careful to control his own. But he was feeling fear, too—fear that he was getting too involved with this single mother and with the little girl he had yet to meet.

"Samantha," he murmured gently, "you can come out, sweetheart. The bad men are gone."

"Prince Sebastian is telling the truth, honey," Jessica added. "They are all gone. And you can hear the sirens. The police are on their way. You're safe."

Something shifted in the shadows, but the child would not come out.

"You're smart," Sebastian praised her. "You have found a very good hiding place. When my brother and I were young boys, we had to hide often from bad men. But we never knew how long to hide before it was safe to come out again. So my father gave us a code word he would use to tell us when it was safe to come out of hiding."

"Sebastian?" Jessica uttered his name in a gasp of surprise over his admission. No one knew about his and Antoine's past. King Omar had kept the true story from the media.

"This code word had to be something that only our father and my brother and I would know. No one else could guess at it then. No one else could trick us to come out of hiding."

Tires squealed as cars stopped in front of the house. But Sebastian's focus remained on the darkness. "So your mother needs to tell you something that only the two of you know. She needs to remind you of a secret only the two of you share, so I will step away now. I will go talk to the policemen and when you're ready to come out, perhaps you can talk to the policemen, too."

He stepped back from the dark, intending to give Jessica and her daughter this moment alone. But just as he turned around, someone moved quickly—coming out of the shadows to clasp his hand.

He stared down at the little girl. Her golden brown hair was tangled around her tear-stained face. Dust and cobwebs clung to her faded jeans and striped shirt. She stared up at him with eyes as wide as her mother's, but instead of the warm brown, hers were a smoky, serious gray.

"You're the prince," she said. "From TV."

Jessica had dropped to her knees in front of her child, her arms winding tight around the girl's small frame. "Thank God you're all right. Thank God you were hiding."

Just because she'd been hiding didn't mean she hadn't heard everything that had happened in her house, to her friend. He entwined his fingers with hers. "You were very smart to do as your mother told you," he praised her again, like he wished his grandfather had once praised either him or Antoine. "But why did you come out before you and your mother shared a secret?"

"We did," the child replied. "You're the secret."

He chuckled. "I'm the secret?"

"You're real," she said, her voice full of awe. "You're a real prince." She glanced at his jeans and boots. "And you're a cowboy, too." She turned toward her mother. "Helen was wrong. Princes can be cowboys."

He opened his mouth to tell her that he was no cowboy. But she was smiling up at him—a smile that lit up her whole face as if sunshine beamed right out of her eyes. And it warmed him from the outside in, straight to his heart.

He had been right to be afraid. He was in too deep with Jessica and with her beautiful, brave little girl. He was falling for them both—and he, better than most, knew that loving someone didn't mean that you would always be able to protect them.

But he vowed then, as he stared down into that little girl's smiling face, that he would try as hard as his father had. And if, like his father, he failed, he would at least die trying.

Chapter Ten

"Helen will be all right, then?" Jessica asked again, needing assurance.

The E.R. doctor, a young dark-haired woman, stood over the bed where an unconscious Helen lay, looking so battered and broken. "She has some broken ribs, a fractured nose and a concussion. We need to keep her for observation because of the concussion. Barring any complications, she will be able to go home within a couple of days."

Home.

Alone.

Guilt clutched at Jessica, stealing her breath. She would not be able to go home with her friend. She couldn't take care of Helen. She and Samantha had to leave. And in the long run, that would be better—safer— for Helen to have her out of her life. Hell, it would have been better for her had Jessica left years ago, or at least weeks ago when all the royals had descended on Dumont with their media coverage and press conferences.

She stepped out of Helen's room and leaned against

the corridor wall, trying to catch her breath. Since finding the door of the ranch house forced open, she hadn't been able to breathe. After several deep breaths, she dug out the cell phone she'd grabbed and shoved into her pocket before Sebastian had driven her and Samantha to the hospital. It wasn't the prince's phone. It was the one she and Helen used on the ranch, and now she punched in one of Helen's preprogrammed numbers.

A gruff voice uttered no greeting, just a, "Damn, woman, you don't need to keep checking on me. I'm fine. It will all work out just fine."

"Mr. McGuire, it's Jessica. Not Helen."

"Jessica?"

"I—I live with Helen."

"Yes, I know who you are, but why are you calling me?" He groaned. "Oh, God, the sirens…I thought they were heading to the resort, that there was more trouble with those damn royals. Guess I should have known Callie would let me know if there was a problem there since she's fallen for one of those visiting sheiks."

Callie was the rancher's daughter and the assistant to the Secretary of Foreign Affairs. She worked out of D.C. but had been born and raised at the Seven M Ranch in Wind River. It was on the other side of the Rattlesnake Badlands from the Double J.

"This doesn't have anything to do with the royals, Mr. McGuire." Even though Prince Sebastian believed otherwise, she knew better. This was all her fault. "Helen's at the hospital."

He audibly sucked in a breath. "She's hurt?"

"Yes, sir. She'll be fine, but they'll be keeping her a couple of days for observation."

"What happened? Horse throw her, or did she cut herself with some power tools?" he asked, then grumbled, "Damn stubborn woman works harder than any man I know."

"I know." She could only hope to be half as strong as Helen Jeffries was. But Helen had once been like her, an abused wife. That was how, at their first meeting in town four years ago, Helen had known what Jessica had been through and how badly she'd needed a friend. "But this wasn't an accident. Helen was attacked and beaten."

Curses rattled the phone. "Who did this? Who hurt her? Did Sheriff Wolf catch them?"

"Not yet."

"I bet this has something to do with the press conference one of those princes held this morning, stirring everything up again."

"Did Helen tell you that I was the witness he was asking to come forward?"

"Helen never tells anyone's business," he defended his lady friend. "I just put it together this morning when I saw his press conference on TV. Before then I never even knew there was a witness. Then it made sense that it was you. You work up at the resort, and that road is the only one between it and the ranch."

So Sebastian was right that whoever was behind that explosion could have figured out she was the witness and come after her because of that. But the sick feeling in the pit of her stomach warned her otherwise.

"None of what has happened around here has really been the royals' fault," she found herself defending them, specifically Prince Sebastian Cavanaugh.

"No," he agreed with a heavy sigh. "But trouble just finds them."

Jessica could see down the hall to the waiting room where Sebastian waited with Samantha. The little girl clung to him, sitting on his lap, her arms wrapped around him. Since climbing out from beneath the stairs, she had not let him go. If not for him, she might still be in her hiding place. He'd reached out to her, not just physically but emotionally. He'd connected to her little girl on a level that Jessica had not been able to.

Because he had lived through a similar situation…

From whom had he and his brother had to hide?

"Is she awake?" Clay asked.

"Helen?" Of course he was talking about Helen. She turned away from the waiting room. "Not yet. She has a concussion, so they've put her in a medical coma to avoid any swelling."

His breath rattled the phone. "Probably a good thing because if she was awake that damn woman would be tracking down the guys who did this herself."

Jessica smiled and agreed. "She probably would."

"I'm on my way, but if she wakes up before I get to the hospital, can you tell her that I, that I…"

Her smile widened. "Yes?"

"Just tell her that I'll be right there, okay?"

It was good that he would because Jessica couldn't be there for her friend. But she wasn't sure that Clay would be, either, in the long run. The two only casually dated. Neither wanted anything deeper or more complicated, or so they claimed.

Jessica understood. She didn't want anything complicated, either, which was all that her feelings for Sebastian were—a complication. They had no future. If Evgeny had found her, as she suspected, then she had no future at all.

"IS THE SHERIFF still out at the ranch?" Sebastian asked, speaking into the cell phone he'd turned on despite the warning on the waiting room wall prohibiting their use. While some of the staff glanced at him, no one tried to enforce the rule. Of course he wasn't the only one breaking it.

Jessica had used her phone already to call one of Helen's friends. Now, while she waited for that friend to arrive, she let Samantha play games on the phone at a table in a corner of the waiting room. But she stayed close to her, as if worried that someone would storm in and grab the child from her arms.

"No, he's left," Antoine replied. "The forensics experts are still here, collecting evidence." And apparently Antoine was overseeing their collection.

"Is Jane there?"

"Yeah, she finished up with your Hummer and came

out to this scene. She'll compare the bullets found here to the slug she pulled from the armrest."

They'd fought earlier over Sebastian not immediately reporting the shooting, but perhaps his brother understood now that he had not been willing to let Jessica out of his sight even then. And now—never...

Or at least not until whoever was after her was apprehended. Then once she was safe, he'd have to let her go. What kind of future could they possibly have with her home in America and his home and responsibilities all in Barajas?

She'd been willing to leave her home out of fear. Would she leave it out of love? Not that he expected her to fall in love with him. Or he with her...

He shook off the wayward thoughts and focused on what was important. "Did they find anything that might lead us to the men in the van?"

"They found the van in the Rattlesnake Badlands," Antoine replied.

"That is where those shots came from."

"You need to go out there with the sheriff or Jane and point out exactly where those shots came from."

"I can't leave Jessica and Samantha."

"They are not your responsibility," Antoine said.

"They're in danger, possibility because my press conference revealed her as the witness. They *are* my responsibility."

Antoine did not argue with him.

"They found the van," he said. "What about the

men?" He would not let Jessica and Samantha out of his sight until they had been apprehended.

"The van was empty and on fire," Antoine replied. "That was how they found it so easily."

"That was how the men destroyed whatever evidence they might have left that would have led to their whereabouts."

"We'll find them," Antoine vowed.

Samantha glanced up from her mother's cell phone and smiled at him—that smile that lit up her face and the entire room and his heart. Her mother stared up at him, too, but her beautiful face was tense, with no smile. And those big eyes of hers were dark and full of fear.

"We have to find them," Sebastian said. Movement near the doorway drew his attention from Jessica and Samantha. "The sheriff's here." He clicked off his cell.

The dark-haired man headed toward Jessica, but Sebastian stepped in front of him. "Sheriff, I need to speak with you."

"You should have called me earlier." Like Antoine, he was apparently not happy that Sebastian hadn't immediately reported the shooting. "Right now I need to talk to Ms. Peters."

"I was there at the ranch, too," Sebastian reminded him.

"I need to talk to her about Helen Jeffries," the sheriff said.

"I doubt this attack had anything to do with Mrs.

Jeffries." From everything Jessica had said about the woman, she seemed like a saint—someone very unlikely to have any enemies.

"I doubt that, too," the sheriff admitted. "Those men were probably looking for Ms. Peters."

Sebastian's guts twisted with dread and fear. "I am certain they were looking for Ms. Peters."

The sheriff nodded in agreement. "Because of what she witnessed."

"You heard what she had to say," Sebastian reminded the lawman. "She didn't see anything that would lead to whoever was behind the explosion. Nor did she see anything that would lead us to Amir's whereabouts."

"Apparently they don't know that."

That was what he had believed, too. But maybe Jessica was right, and there was someone else after her. Some monster from her past…

A WEIGHT DESCENDED on Jessica's chest, stealing the breath from her lungs. She couldn't inhale from the mass she was suffocating under, the pressure bearing on her to run. Before it was too late…

But she couldn't drag her gaze from the man standing on the other side of the room. Even though he was deep in conversation with the sheriff, he kept his implacable stare on her, as if unwilling to let her out of his sight.

Then he walked away from the sheriff and crossed the room toward her and Samantha. The little girl vaulted out of her chair and launched herself at Sebastian, climbing up his body and into his arms.

Jessica understood her daughter's reaction. She wanted to crawl into his arms herself, but she couldn't afford the luxury of dumping all her problems on someone else. Doing that to Helen could have cost the woman her life.

"Sheriff Wolf would like to talk to you," Sebastian said.

"Me or…" She glanced at Samantha's face. The child hadn't said anything about what she'd heard while she'd been hiding in the closet, and Jessica hadn't wanted to ask her until the child was ready to talk. She also suspected that she was not the person who should talk to Samantha about that. Neither was the sheriff.

He shook his head. "He'll ask Helen about what happened."

The little girl shivered when he said her friend's name. Jessica had been careful that her daughter not see how badly Helen had been injured. She'd kept her in the kitchen until the ambulance had carried Helen to the hospital. Jessica had assured the little girl that the woman was fine but that the doctors were just being extra careful because Helen was so special.

"Then why does he want to talk to me?" Jessica asked. She didn't want to sit for another inquisition like she had at the resort. Once Clay arrived at the hospital to be with Helen, she intended to take Samantha and leave Wind River forever.

"He wants your statement about what happened at the ranch," he replied. "We took off after the ambulance before he had a chance to talk to us."

"He didn't talk to you very long," she observed.

"I didn't have as much to tell him as you do," he said.

Her gaze slipped from his handsome face down to her daughter's. "You want me to tell him about…"

"If you really believe he's the one behind what happened today…"

Maybe she had jumped to conclusions. Maybe those men were only after her because of what she'd witnessed and it had nothing to do with Evgeny.

"I don't know what to believe right now," she admitted as exhaustion tugged at every muscle, weighing them down so that it took effort for her to rise from her chair.

"You can believe me," he said. "You can believe that I will protect you and Samantha."

She wanted to point out that he hadn't even been able to protect his own friend from the explosion, but she couldn't be that cruel. And it would be cruel because she knew how protective Sebastian was; it had to be killing him that his friend had been hurt, or maybe worse, and he hadn't been able to help him.

"I'll talk to the sheriff," she agreed.

"You'll tell him about…?" He glanced down at Samantha, who rested her head against his broad shoulder, as Jessica longed to do. They were being careful to avoid particulars while they talked, but the child must have picked up on the tone of their conversation. And probably on Jessica's fear.

Had she let that fear make her irrational? Of course there was no doubt they were in danger, and she would be more foolish to not be afraid.

But she shrugged. "I don't know. It's been five years. Maybe there's nothing to tell the sheriff."

"Teresa!"

The shout—and the voice—drew her attention to the door. And to the man who'd just walked into the waiting room. Both the name and the man were from her past. If only they would have stayed there…

But as it all washed over her—all the pain and fear—hysteria rose and then bubbled out of her throat in a scream.

Chapter Eleven

Jessica's scream echoed throughout the room and in Sebastian's head, like other screams that sometimes haunted him. Samantha clutched him tighter, burying her little face in his neck as she trembled in his arms. While he patted her back with one hand, he reached for her mother with the other, needing to protect her.

Her scream and wide-eyed look of horror told him who had entered the waiting room even before he turned toward the doorway. Evgeny Surinka walked in alone, without the men Jessica was so certain he had sent ahead to grab her. He didn't need to hire muscle. The man was built like a boxer, with heavy arms that strained the sleeves of his gray suit, and his hands, which he fisted at his sides, were the size of dinner plates.

Thinking of those fists striking Jessica sent rage coursing through Sebastian, heating his blood. If Samantha wasn't clinging to him, he would have launched himself at Evgeny. All he could do now was step between Jessica and the man who'd abused her physically so long ago and had continued to do so emotionally and mentally even after she'd run away from him.

Evgeny narrowed his eyes, which were the same gray as Samantha's. But while hers sparkled with warmth and friendliness, his were as cold and hard as the metal of the gun Sebastian wanted to thrust in his face. As if sensing his murderous intent, the man sucked in an audible breath. But he wasn't looking at Sebastian anymore; he stared instead at the child in Sebastian's arms.

"Teresa, is this my daughter?"

Jessica stepped out from behind Sebastian. "No."

"Why do I suspect a DNA test will say otherwise?" he challenged her.

"You're not the only one with suspicions, Surinka," Sebastian said.

"You know my name," Evgeny said, and an evil grin curved his thin lips. "You have me at a disadvantage then because I do not know you." The condescending glint in his eyes claimed otherwise.

"I am Prince Sebastian Cavanaugh."

"The one who held the press conference this morning," he said, his gaze skimming over Sebastian's shirt and jeans. "I didn't recognize you." He turned back to Jessica. "But I recognized *you*."

"She was not there this morning."

"She must have showed up later—for the reward," Evgeny said. "Or at least that's what the reporters speculated when you chased her out of the Wind River County Courthouse."

"Were you here this morning?" Sebastian asked.

Evgeny tilted his head again, his jaw clenching, as if he struggled to control his anger over being interrogated. "My plane just flew in," he said. "Only booked my flight after I caught that glimpse of Teresa." He kept staring at her, his gaze so possessive. "Despite the red dye and the straight hair, I knew it was you."

She shivered, and Sebastian wrapped his free arm around her shoulders. But she tensed in his loose embrace and shrugged off his arm. "No, you're wrong. My name's not Teresa." She shook her head, even more desperately denying her identity than she'd denied being the witness. "I'm not who you think I am."

"It's been five years," Evgeny said, "but I would know you anywhere, Teresa." He reached a hand toward her, but she flinched and stepped back. "You can't deny who you are." The flinch had given her away because triumph leaped in his cold gray eyes. "You're my wife."

"No." She shook her head again but not in denial of her identity because she added, "I filed papers. I'm not your wife any longer."

"You filed while I was in prison," he said, his voice hard with that barely suppressed rage. "But you never signed the papers."

"You didn't give her the chance," Sebastian said. He pressed his hand over the little girl's ear that wasn't nestled into his neck. "You put her in the hospital."

"I have no idea what you're talking about," Evgeny said. "Or even *why* you're talking. This should be a private conversation between a man and his wife." He glanced toward the child, but he couldn't see her face because Sebastian kept his hand there, protecting her from the cold hard gaze of her father. "And my daughter."

"She's not yours," Jessica said, her voice just a shaky whisper. She reached for Samantha, prying the trembling child from Sebastian's arms. Then she turned away, in the direction where the sheriff waited to speak with her and stood watching them, his eyes narrowed as he tried to figure out what was going on.

But Evgeny reached out and grabbed her arm. "You're not getting away from me again."

Sebastian wrapped his hand around the Russian's wrist and squeezed until Evgeny eased his grip. And Jessica tugged free and crossed the room, taking herself and her child out of the ruthless man's reach.

"You are going to talk to me," Evgeny yelled after his wife. He shrugged off Sebastian's hand and started toward Jessica.

But Sebastian blocked him and the man shoved against his chest, trying to move him. Sebastian was immovable, though, with his legs planted apart and rage coursing through his veins. He wanted the man to swing at him so that he didn't have to swing first.

"The only one you should be talking to is the sheriff," Sebastian said. "You have some questions to answer."

"About what?" Evgeny asked as he stepped back.

"About what happened today—at the resort and out at the ranch." And maybe even on that ridge. While his men had been in the van, Evgeny could have been in the badlands.

That evil smirk crossed the man's face, but he shrugged off Sebastian's accusations. "I have no idea what you're talking about."

"Neither do I," said Sheriff Wolf.

Sebastian had been so focused on Evgeny that he hadn't noticed when the lawman had joined them. Like him, the man had braced himself as if ready for a fight— or at least ready to break one up.

"You need to be questioning him about the men who attacked Helen Jeffries," Sebastian said. "They probably work for him."

"What men?" Evgeny asked, glancing around the waiting room as if expecting to find them. But the waiting room was not very crowded—only a few other people sat on chairs that faced the television. But they didn't even pretend to be watching it; instead they watched them. "I just arrived in town."

"But you sent your men ahead to find Jessica."

"Teresa," Evgeny corrected him. "And I did no such thing." He turned toward the sheriff. "You have no reason to question me."

"Forget about questioning him, then, and just arrest him," Sebastian advised.

"For what?" Evgeny asked, arching a pale blond brow. "There are no outstanding warrants against me. I've even served out my parole."

"You violated your parole when you got out of prison

and beat your wife." Sebastian fisted his hands, ready to beat the man who'd been so vicious to a woman who deserved only respect and tenderness.

"I don't know what she told you," Evgeny said, "but that's not what she told anyone else. She never pressed charges against me."

"She was too scared to do that," Sebastian defended her. "Then. Talk to her now, Sheriff. She'll tell you all about her ex-husband."

Sheriff Wolf glanced across the room to where Jessica stood with her daughter and then back to the men who stood uncomfortably close to each other. "Can I leave you two over here without worrying you'll beat the hell out of each other?"

"Maybe not," Sebastian acknowledged. He really, really wanted—no, hell, he *needed*—to make Evgeny Surinka feel the pain and fear he'd subjected Jessica to for years.

Evgeny chuckled and held up his hands. "I want no trouble. I only came here to bring my wife—" his throat moved as he swallowed hard "—and child home with me."

"They're not going anywhere with you," Sebastian said. "Sheriff, please, talk to Jessica."

"Teresa," Evgeny corrected him again. The sheriff only nodded and walked over to her and Samantha. Evgeny turned to Sebastian and reiterated, "Her name is Teresa."

"Not anymore. That woman you knew—your wife— she's gone. You killed her five years ago."

Evgeny laughed. "How long have you known my wife?"

Sebastian lifted his chin. "It doesn't matter how long. It's how well."

"You don't know her very well at all," Evgeny said. "She and I grew up together. Her brother and I were best friends. We've known each other most of our lives. We are connected in a way that you will never know or experience. I don't know what she told you in order to gain your sympathy and probably a lot of your money, but I do know that she will come back to me."

"She stayed away from you for five years," Sebastian reminded the narcissist. "If your men hadn't hurt her friend, she would already be gone. She knew it was you behind everything." And Sebastian should have trusted her and helped her get away before Evgeny had found out about Samantha. And before Jessica had had to face the monster from her past.

Evgeny laughed again. "She'd be gone…with your big reward money, man. Haven't you figured out that she's been playing you all along?"

Sebastian shook his head in disgust. "You are un- believable."

"You'd be smart to believe me," Evgeny said, "be- cause as I already told you, I know the real Teresa."

"Jessica," Sebastian murmured.

"Let me guess," Evgeny continued as if he hadn't

spoken, "Teresa claimed to be that witness you're look-ing for, but then she really had nothing to tell you about that night that you didn't already know."

He shook his head.

"So I'm wrong?" That pale blond brow arched again. "She led you to your missing friend?"

"You're wrong about her wanting my money," he said. "She refused to accept the reward."

"Of course she did," Evgeny said, "which made you all the more determined to give her that money and anything else. Oh, and then when she shared her sob story with you, she really roped you in, got you all de-termined to take care of her. To protect her." Evgeny reached out and patted his shoulder in commiseration. "She does that to a man, plays all vulnerable so that he wants to protect her."

Sebastian itched to slam his fist into the man's smug face. Instead he forced a laugh, too. "Better men than you have tried to mess with my head. It's not going to work."

Not again. But it had worked once. Even though he was dead, his grandfather still lived in Sebastian's mind—haunting him with all his criticisms and com-plaints. It wouldn't have mattered what Sebastian had done; it never would have been good enough for King Omar Zubira because he'd never been good enough. Because Omar hadn't believed Sebastian's father had been good enough to marry his daughter. And in the end maybe he hadn't been.

"I am going to protect her from you," Sebastian vowed.

Evgeny chuckled. "That's funny, really, when you're the one who actually needs protecting."

JESSICA COULDN'T SPEAK, could only nod or shake her head in response to the sheriff's questions. She didn't care as much about what he was saying as she worried about what Evgeny was saying to Sebastian.

Better than anyone, she knew how the man could manipulate someone. Heck, even as a young boy he'd been able to manipulate people into feeling things they hadn't felt, into believing things they'd always doubted.

"I'm not lying," she said.

"About what?" the sheriff asked, his brow furrowed with confusion.

"He's a bad man," she said, glancing back at her daughter. Samantha sat at that table again, far enough away from her mother and her father that she wouldn't be able to hear either conversation—especially because she was listening to the MP3 player again.

"I can't arrest him for that," Wolf replied. "You'll have to swear out a complaint against him."

"For something he did five years ago?" she asked. "In another state? Can you arrest him?"

"We can work with the police department where the crime occurred."

She snorted. "He works with the police department where the crime occurred."

"He's a cop?"

"He's more powerful than that."

"What is he?" Wolf asked, with another glance over his shoulder at the men who stood too close together and were too deep in conversation.

"An FBI informant. That's how he got out of prison. He turned over evidence against someone the Feds wanted for a long time."

"Who?" Wolf asked.

"His father." He'd turned against the man he'd both feared and loved—because of her. Once she'd served him with the divorce papers, he'd been determined to get to her at whatever cost. And no one would get in his way or stop him.

Sebastian had promised her that he would, but she couldn't count on him. She couldn't count on anyone. But she could count on Evgeny never giving up.

"So you think that because of what he's done for the FBI, he's untouchable?" the sheriff asked.

"I've been gone for five years," she said. "Maybe things have changed. Maybe he got in trouble again."

"I'll do what Prince Sebastian suggested and search for outstanding warrants."

"I wish you could arrest him."

"Unless there's a warrant for him, I wouldn't be able to hold him."

"Even if you could hold him for just a little while…" Giving her enough time to run away with Samantha.

"I'll see what I can do." The sheriff pulled out his

cell phone, then glanced at the sign prohibiting its use. "I'll be right back," he assured her as he walked toward the hall.

Sebastian followed him out, his deep voice vibrating with anger. Her own temper flared as she realized they'd left her and Samantha alone with Evgeny.

As he walked over to her, a grin curved his cruel lips. Instead of running away or cowering, she met him halfway, stepping between him and Samantha as Sebastian had stepped in front of her just a short while ago.

"You're losing your white knight," Evgeny taunted her.

"What did you say to him?"

"I told him he was wasting his time with you," he replied. "That you and I have a connection that will never be broken."

She glanced back at Samantha, making sure the little girl still had the phone pressed to her ear, listening to music. Still, Jessica pitched her voice lower, so her child would not overhear. "You broke that connection when you broke my nose as well as a couple other of my bones five years ago."

"I didn't want to hurt you. But you'd made me so angry, trying to leave me."

"That was no excuse—"

"You know that I have an excuse, though. You know how I was raised," Evgeny reminded her.

All those times he'd come to their apartment, battered from his father's fists, flashed through her mind. The sympathy she'd felt for him then had become something more once they'd grown up. It had turned to love. But then Evgeny had turned into someone else, the man he'd claimed to hate.

"Then you," she replied, "should know better than anyone how it feels to be treated that way."

"See, Teresa," he said, with that wicked grin that always used to charm her, "you understand me—as no one else ever has."

"I know you," she said. "But I don't understand you at all."

"No." He shook his head and reached for her, but when she flinched, he fisted his hands at his sides. "You and I share that special connection."

"And I told you that you severed that—"

"I'm talking about our daughter," he said. "She's the connection we'll always have."

"She's not yours," she hotly denied.

He laughed. "You cannot deny her paternity. She looks just like me. I am her father."

But for her eyes, she had actually looked more like Sebastian when he'd held her—as a father would, with comfort and care. Evgeny would never care about anyone as much as he cared about himself.

"You'll have to order a DNA test to prove that," she said because she would never admit it. And his lawyer would have to track her down to serve her with the court order to have it done.

"You have changed," Evgeny admitted. "You're not the same woman I remember."

She expelled a shaky breath. "I'm not." She wasn't the naive young girl who'd fallen for his charm and his lies and his sad story. "You need to let me go."

His jaw clenched, a muscle jumping in his cheek. "You can try to run again," he said. "But you're not taking her with you. What did you name her?"

He asked as if he intended to change the child's name if he didn't like it. She lifted her chin. "You don't need to know her name because you're never going to get to know her."

He leaned closer, his gray eyes hard with rage, and in a vicious whisper demanded, "Tell me her name."

The fear he always filled her with, even when he was hundreds of miles away, gripped her and had her automatically obeying him. "Samantha. Her name is Samantha."

He expelled a ragged breath. "For your brother." He nodded. "I understand…"

"I don't care if you understand. I don't care what you think, either." Her anger and mother's instincts of protection beat back her fear. "You're not going to be part of her life."

"I'm not just going for a DNA test. I'm going for full custody. You've stolen over four years of her life from me. I'll take the rest from you."

He threatened more than a custody battle, and she knew it. He threatened more than her life even; he threatened to take away her very reason for living. Jessica's stomach pitched as she realized her worst nightmare was about to come true.

DMITRI DUCKED HIS CHIN into the collar of his coat, hoping nobody recognized him. "We shouldn't have come back here," he murmured to the driver who hunched low behind the wheel of the small SUV they'd rented days ago as a backup to the van.

"The boss ordered it," the driver reminded him. "Said we can't take our eyes off her or she'll split again."

"We shouldn't be hanging around here, not after what we…" Bile rose in his throat. He hadn't wanted to hurt the older woman, but she'd damn near killed him. He rubbed at his shoulder and winced. He'd dug out the buckshot, but the wounds were raw, like the ones on his face where the woman had clawed his skin.

"We needed to know if that red-haired woman was the woman the boss has been looking for," the driver replied. "And now we know."

"That ranch lady didn't tell us, though," Dmitri reminded him with a flash of respect despite his pain.

"She is a loyal friend," the driver grudgingly admitted.

"She probably has more than one here. We should not be here. Especially *here*." He glanced around the parking lot, hoping no one had noticed them. While they sat in the dark, steam had begun to build up on the windows. "I wish Rurik had not recognized the woman.

If he hadn't, we'd never have had to come to this god-forsaken place. Look what happened to Rurik after he came here."

"He got killed," Nic recalled with a shudder. "Crushed to death."

"After he murdered someone," Dmitri added. He'd first met the man in prison, years ago in Russia. Then they had met again, years later, through the boss. Rurik hadn't been on the payroll, though. He'd been a contract killer.

Live by the sword, die by the sword.

Dmitri shuddered, too. "And all hell broke loose around here. Now is not the time for us to be here, not when it's crawling with cops and reporters. We need to leave."

"And disobey a direct order?" Nic shook his head. "I do not want to be on the boss's bad side."

"He does not have a good side." Dmitri feared that he would wind up just like Rurik. Dead. But he probably would not be the only one. If the boss was going down, he would not go alone.

Chapter Twelve

Sebastian stared out into the night. Fog had rolled in and he could see nothing outside the lodge. Inside, he saw too much. His reflection bounced back from the dark glass, but he didn't look at his own image. Instead he stared beyond himself, through the open door to the other bedroom in the suite. He'd left it open so he could make sure that Jessica didn't try to run.

Even though he couldn't see out, he knew that Evgeny and his men waited out there, ready to catch her should she try to escape.

Escape?

He pushed his hand through his hair, disgusted with himself. Escape from whom? Him? Had he become as bad as Evgeny—determined to hang on to her no matter what she wanted?

She hadn't wanted to come back to the resort with him, but the sheriff and Samantha had both urged her to accept his invitation. Hell, it hadn't been an invitation at all. He'd ordered her to come back to his suite so that he could protect her from Evgeny.

But who would protect her from him?

How could he save her without scaring her more? Without convincing her that he was exactly like the man who'd abused her?

He moved away from the window, drawn to that open door. She lay in the bed with her daughter, her arms wrapped tight around Samantha as if afraid that Evgeny would break in and try to wrest the child from her arms as they lay sleeping. Perhaps she was right to be afraid. That seemed exactly like something the ruthless Russian would do.

Sebastian could be ruthless, too. He'd proven that every time he'd pulled the trigger. He could protect Jessica and Samantha. He would not fail like his father had failed his mother.

She shifted on the mattress, and a pang of guilt struck him that he violated her privacy in watching them sleep. He had no right.

He had no rights at all where Jessica was concerned. But when he turned away, she called out, a soft cry that reached inside him and squeezed his heart. He didn't remember moving, but he was at her side, kneeling beside the bed.

She cried out again, and Samantha murmured, drawn awake by her mother's fear.

"Shh," he soothed the child back to sleep.

The woman was not soothed. Instead her eyes opened, wide with fear, and her mouth opened, a scream on her lips. He could have silenced Jessica with his palm, but almost every time he reached a hand toward her, she flinched. So he silenced her with his mouth instead. He pressed his lips to hers.

She lifted her hands to his hair and he winced, expecting that she would pull him away. Instead she tunneled her fingers into it and clutched him to her.

"I knew he was a real prince," Samantha murmured.

Sebastian jerked away from her mother while Jessica's face flushed bright red. She'd been asleep when he'd kissed her; she had no reason to be embarrassed. He was the one who'd been awake and aware of what he was doing.

Kissing her…

His lips tingled and he could still taste her.

"Are you a princess now, Mommy?" Samantha asked, rubbing her knuckles into her sleep-dazed eyes. "Since he kissed you?"

"No, honey. I'm not a princess. You're dreaming, sweetie," Jessica said, pressing a kiss to her daughter's forehead. "Go back to sleep." She tugged the blanket over the little girl's shoulders, and then she slipped out of the bed and motioned Sebastian to follow her from the room. She wore one of the hotel robes, which was velvety soft and in a rich gold color that brought out the golden tone of her skin.

Did she wear anything beneath it? He wanted to reach for the belt of the robe, but she beat him there, tightening it around her waist.

"You were dreaming, too," he said after she pulled the door almost closed behind them.

"You didn't kiss me?" she asked with a slight smile.

"Oh, I did that. But you were dreaming before I kissed you. You cried out."

"I was having a nightmare," she admitted with a shiver.

"About Evgeny taking Samantha away."

"Yes." She shuddered now. "And about what happened today to Helen."

"She's going to be okay."

"Will Samantha? She was there when that happened. She was hiding, but the walls in the old house are thin. She could have heard everything that happened. Will she be okay?"

"Why are you asking me? I am not the person to ask," he replied. "I don't know anything about kids." He hadn't been one since that awful night when his father hadn't come for him and Antoine. His gut clenched as the dark descended over him again. He turned back toward the window, but he still couldn't see out. He could only see inside—to the past.

A hand, small but rough with calluses, slid over his, entwined their fingers and tugged him back around to face her. Her dark eyes warm with sympathy, she stared up at him.

"You know why I'm asking you. Ever since you commiserated with Samantha, I've been dying to ask you…

how you could. How did you know everything that my little girl was feeling today?"

"You know why," he said, "because I felt it, too."

"How old were you?"

"Six—almost seven. But I don't remember how old Antoine and I were when Dad first taught us how to play hide and don't come out until he gave us the safe word."

"Was he concerned that people were going to come after you because you're royalty? You and your brother were probably at great risk of being kidnapped and held for ransom."

If only money had been what those people had wanted...

He shook his head. "Revenge."

"Held for revenge?"

"My father was Special Forces. He'd made a lot of enemies over the years—enemies who had wanted to see him suffer. A lot."

She glanced to that closed door. "And nothing makes a parent suffer more than hurting their child."

"He won't get her," Sebastian assured her. Taking advantage of their entwined fingers, he tugged her closer so that she pressed against his chest. And he closed his arms around her.

She drew in a deep breath that lifted her soft breasts in that soft robe. Then she expelled the breath and relaxed against him. "The men who wanted to get revenge on your father, they didn't get you and your brother. Samantha could be safe."

He tightened his arms around her. She had shared so much with him today that it was only fair he do the same. "They didn't get me and my brother, but…"

She stilled against him. "Oh, my God…"

"But—" he forced himself to continue "—they got my mother. That's how I know what Samantha heard today…because Antoine and I heard everything from where we were hiding."

Her arms slid around his back and squeezed. "I'm so sorry."

"And he…" He stopped to clear the emotion from his throat. "He never came to get us out of our hiding place."

She gasped. "Your father, too?"

"He died trying to protect our mother." But he had failed. Would Sebastian? Was he the right person to try to save Jessica?

"And you and your brother. He saved the two of you," she said. "He saved his sons."

"It was his job to protect my mother, you know. Grandfather had hired him to be her bodyguard. After he'd left Special Forces, he'd been a mercenary. King Omar was willing to pay any price to keep his only child safe. While he'd been worried about her physical safety, he should have been worried about her emotional safety. She fell for my father." Tom Cavanaugh had been an impressive man: over six-and-a-half-feet-tall with muscles and tattoos and scars, and golden blond hair and blue eyes. He'd been his and Antoine's hero as well as their father. "But King Omar would not approve their marriage. In fact he forbade it, so they ran off and eloped."

"Why wouldn't he approve? Because your father was a mercenary? You said he was in Special Forces before that. Was he American?"

Sebastian nodded.

"So you're half American?"

He shrugged. "Grandfather never acknowledged that half of us. After we came to live with him, he never allowed us to talk about our father." That hadn't stopped him, though, from constantly comparing them to their failure of a father. He'd been so angry and bitter over the senseless loss of his only child. "Most people don't know what happened or that we are, as Grandfather said, half commoner."

"So he didn't approve of your father because he was American?"

"Because he wasn't royalty," Sebastian explained. "Grandfather was not prejudiced about nationality. He married a European princess himself. He believed royalty should marry only royalty."

She flinched as if he'd reached for her. But he hadn't lifted his hands from his sides. "So he was a snob."

Sebastian shrugged. "I don't know. I think he was just realistic. And he was right about my father being the wrong man to marry a princess."

"Your father loved her, and he loved you," she said in defense of a man she'd never met. "He taught you and your brother to hide from danger. What was the safe word he used for you to come out?"

"Oreos."

"What?"

"He'd sneak 'em to us even though Mother didn't approve of us having sweets—said that they made us too hyper. So Dad would sneak us cookies. It was our secret with him—one even she didn't know."

She squeezed his arm. "You loved him so much."

He hadn't realized that he had. He'd almost let Grandfather's bitterness eradicate all the good memories. If only there had been more…

"He never prepared us for him not coming for us," Sebastian admitted.

"How long did you two stay in hiding?"

"Too long," he admitted with a heavy sigh. "If we'd come out sooner and called for help, we might have been able to save them."

She shook her head. "Or you two might have been killed, too. You did the right thing, remaining hidden. You both must have been so scared." She sucked in a shaky breath. "Like Samantha must have been so scared today." She glanced out the window to where the sky was beginning to lighten behind the fog. "Yesterday."

"She's fine now. But you have to make sure she sees Helen and knows that she's fine, too," he said. "After what she heard she will need that assurance."

She nodded. "Of course. I didn't let her see Helen earlier because of the blood and the swelling."

"And that was the right thing to do." Because he could never get out of his head those images he'd seen once he and Antoine had come out of the darkness. They would haunt him forever. "But she will need to see her before you go running off like you planned."

She stepped back from him. "I need to run."

"I can't let you do that," he said. And even at the risk of sounding like Evgeny, he had to add, "I can't let you leave."

JESSICA SHIVERED. Her white knight hadn't taken off, as Evgeny had insinuated at the hospital; instead he'd taken over, bustling her and Samantha back to the resort and his private suite.

"Go back to bed," he said, issuing another of his autocratic orders. "You're cold."

It wasn't the cool temperature in the room chilling her skin; it was his demeanor. And who it reminded her of. Was she forever doomed to be attracted to the wrong kind of man?

"I should call the hospital and check on Helen," she said, crossing the room to the phone.

"That's a good idea," Sebastian said. "I'll give you some time alone."

She suspected that after what he had just shared with her, he was the one who needed time alone. So she watched him leave the room and waited until he closed the door to the hall before dialing the phone. She could have called a cab to take her and Samantha to the train station because he was gone and wouldn't have overheard.

But instead she called Helen. A gruff male voice answered, "Hello?"

"Mr. McGuire, it's Jessica Peters," she identified herself. "How is she?"

"There was no swelling in her brain, so they woke her up from the coma. She talked to the sheriff and gave him descriptions of the two guys who attacked her. Wolf said they matched descriptions you gave of the two guys who tried grabbing you at the resort." Clay's deep voice vibrated with concern. "What's going on, Jessica?"

"I'm sorry," she murmured. "Tell Helen I'm sorry."

"Jessica, if you need help…"

"She gave me help. That's why she got hurt," Jessica said. "I don't want her to get hurt any more."

"She won't. I'm not leaving her side, visiting hours be damned. She's in danger, and I'm going to protect her no matter how hard the damn stubborn woman fights me." He chuckled. "Hell, I'm going to ask her to marry me."

"Which one of us has got the concussion?" a groggy voice murmured in the background.

Jessica's heart clutched with regret.

Clay chuckled with relief and affection. "She's awake. Do you want to talk to her?"

More than anything, Jessica needed her friend. "No, let her rest. I'll bring Samantha to see her tomorrow."

She glanced to the window and the lightening sky. "Later today."

Then, no matter what Sebastian said, she was leaving Wind River County.

"THIS IS A DANGEROUS PLAN," Antoine said as he paced the floor of his suite. It was adjacent to Sebastian's, and the door to the hall was open so that he could hear if Jessica tried to run.

"Yes," Sebastian agreed. "It is very dangerous."

Antoine stopped pacing and stared at him, his light blue eyes full of concern. "You're going to get yourself killed."

"Perhaps."

"Protecting her is not going to bring back our mother."

"No."

"You're not Dad, no matter how much Omar tried to convince you that you are."

"Then I should not get myself killed."

"Sebastian!" Antoine's temper snapped. "Do not be flippant."

"I'm not. I'm scared," he admitted, an admission he had not made since they'd cowered together in that closet so long ago. "But I don't know what else to do."

Antoine sighed. "You can't let them go."

"No, I can't."

"It's not in your nature to walk away from someone who needs help or protection. You always feel responsible for everyone else's safety. That's why you're such a good leader."

Sebastian blew out a breath of surprise. His brother had never been so vocal before, certainly not with praise.

"And because you're such a good leader," Antoine continued, "you can't go getting yourself killed."

"You really don't want to rule Barajas alone," he joked.

Antoine cursed him again.

Sebastian held up his palms to ward off the vulgar insults. "Don't worry, getting killed is not part of my plan."

A muscle twitched in Antoine's cheek. "You can't count on everything going according to plan."

"No, I can't." The last time everything was supposed to go according to plan, he'd wound up in the dark waiting for a safe word that never came, and screams ringing in his ears. This plan could not go that wrong. But his brother was right to be concerned. Sebastian was certain that someone was going to end up dead.

Chapter Thirteen

"You cannot keep me here," she said. "I am not one of your subjects. I am an American citizen, free to come and go as I please."

He stared down at her, his blue gaze unsettlingly intent; his jaw clenched so tightly. "You are a fool to leave here, to leave my protection."

Juggling the blanket-wrapped bundle in her arms, she pulled open the back door and snapped her sleeping child into the booster-style car seat. Then she quickly shut that door and jerked open the driver's side.

"I don't want your protection," she said. "You're no better than he is."

"And you're an even bigger fool than I suspected you were."

She lifted her hand to slap him, but he caught her wrist.

"Your husband warned me that *I* actually needed protection from you," he said. "Apparently I should have heeded his advice…because you refuse to heed mine."

"You didn't offer advice," she said, tugging free of his grasp. "You issued orders. I've had enough of being bullied. No more. If you want to boss people around, I suggest you go back to your own damn country where they have to listen to you."

"Perhaps I shall."

She slid into the driver's seat, and with shaking hands, grasped the steering wheel. "Have a safe trip home, then."

Sebastian grabbed the door before she could shut it, as he had back at the courthouse just the day before. Had it been only a day since she'd met him? It felt like a lifetime ago.

Given how short her life might be, maybe it had been a lifetime.

"Don't forget that I warned you," he said before slamming the door shut for her.

She twisted the key in the ignition. As it had at the courthouse, the motor actually started on the first try. Her stomach clenched with regret and nerves.

This is crazy...

"Damn Antoine. He always has to have the last word," Sebastian said; his deep voice vibrated behind the seats where he crouched on the floor.

"He seems to believe it might actually be the last word he speaks to you." For even though Antoine, posing as his twin, had said the words to her, she knew he'd meant them for Sebastian. His brother was as skeptical of the plan as she was, probably partially because he had been enlisted to protect Samantha. Her little girl was not inside that bundle of blankets she'd buckled into the car seat. She was waiting inside the resort for her temporary guardian.

Prince Antoine Cavanaugh as a babysitter?

Jessica could not believe she had entrusted him with her sweet little girl. But Samantha had not been scared of him, probably because he looked almost exactly like Sebastian except for his eyes. Not only were they a lighter blue but they were also full of cynicism. Despite everything that Sebastian had been through, he was not a cynic. In fact he was more of an optimist than she could ever be because he actually believed his plan could work.

THIS IS NOT GOING TO WORK…

Sebastian studied the ranch through the small circle of the scope he'd taken off his long rifle. Kate, the gun, was there, too—the Remington propped in the corner of the kitchen. Except for a rabbit and some birds, nothing moved outside. Not even the men Antoine had sent ahead to guard the perimeter of the ranch. Were Brenner and the others out there?

Antoine had sworn they were all trustworthy, after he'd interrogated them. If not for his twin vouching for Brenner and the other members of their Barajas security detail, Sebastian never would have allowed Jessica back on the ranch. It had been cleared as a crime scene, all the evidence collected and forwarded to the lab, thanks to Jane's fast work as the forensics expert. The front door had been replaced, but the house still needed to be cleaned up.

"I still wish you would have let a cop pose as you," he said. Jane had offered despite Prince Stefan's protest.

His original plan had had Jessica and Samantha both safe with Antoine at the resort while he and Jane or a deputy, posing as Jessica, flushed out Evgeny.

Jessica sighed, and her breath whispered across the back of his arm as she stood beside him, staring out the window. "That wouldn't have worked."

"Why? You think Evgeny got to someone in the sheriff's office?"

"You must think it's possible or you would have brought Sheriff Wolf in on your little plan."

He sighed now. "I would have, had you agreed to let a female deputy pose as you."

"Evgeny wouldn't have fallen for it," she said. "I grew out my hair, straightened and dyed it, changed the way I walk and talk, and from just a glimpse of me on a news clip, he knew it was me. He would damn well know if it *wasn't* me."

"You sure he knows it's you?" he asked, gesturing toward the stillness outside. "We've been here a couple of days, and he hasn't made a move, not even to send his men ahead." She'd been going out to feed the animals, making sure she'd be seen if anyone was watching the ranch.

"Patience isn't your strong suit?"

He flashed back to all the waiting he'd done in the military, waiting for that perfect shot. It hadn't bothered him then because he'd been waiting alone. It was waiting with someone that sent him back to his dark past, to the time he'd spent in the hiding place with Antoine.

But waiting with Jessica was even worse than the dark because there was nothing to distract him from his attraction to her. Every time she moved, every time she breathed he wanted her more. "Patience used to be one of my attributes."

"It's never been one of mine," she admitted. "And this waiting is killing me. I've never been away from Samantha before."

"Do you want to call her again?" he asked, pulling the untraceable cell phone from his pocket. He and Antoine were both using them, just in case Evgeny tried tapping their phone lines. His twin and the little girl were playing games and watching cartoons in Antoine's suite, on which he'd placed a Do Not Disturb order so that the hotel staff would not see her.

"And interrupt her fun with *Uncle Antoine?*" she asked with a derisive snort.

"Yeah, sorry about that," he said with not much sincerity. "But she needed something to call him."

"I think your brother would have preferred Prince Antoine or maybe Your Highness."

"And that's precisely why I told her to call him uncle," Sebastian admitted, chuckling as he remembered the annoyance that had crossed his brother's face.

"Well, at least she's having fun."

"You're not?" he teased.

"Waiting for someone to try to kill me? Yeah, it's great fun." All the color drained from her face, and her mouth fell open with a gasp. "I'm sorry. I shouldn't have said that. It was so insensitive…after what you told me about…"

"I shouldn't have told you about that," he said, wishing he could take back the confidence he'd shared with her. He'd told her too much; he could tell from the way she avoided looking at him the past couple of days that he'd made her uncomfortable.

"Have you ever told anyone?" she asked.

He shook his head.

"At least you have your brother."

"Your brother is dead," he remembered. "How did that happen?"

"He was murdered," she said almost matter-of-factly. But from what she'd revealed about their lives, she hadn't had an easy upbringing, either. "He was a bouncer at one of Evgeny's father's clubs. He got in a scuffle with someone, and they stabbed him."

"Were they arrested?"

She shook her head. "No. Evgeny promised he'd find his killer. He also promised he'd take care of me. He said that, with his last breath, Sam had asked him to do that. He told me that Sam wanted the two of us to be together. That was when I accepted his marriage proposal." She sighed. "I thought I loved him. Maybe I was just scared to be alone. The way we grew up—with our mom's drug problems—Sam and I had only each other to count on. Losing him was…"

"Like losing your father, your mother and your brother."

"So you're lucky you have your brother."

"Yes, I am." It was good they'd stayed in the dark, even though it still haunted him that they might have been able to save their parents had they come out sooner. "Antoine and I have never talked about what happened," he admitted.

"But…"

"Talking about it means reliving it," he explained.

"I never talk about…Evgeny, either," she said. "But just because I haven't talked about him doesn't mean that I haven't relived what happened with him—all the time inside my head."

And that was why he had to control his desire for her. She'd been through too much to ever trust again.

"I'm sorry that I asked you to do this," he replied. "Maybe you were right to run."

"And you were right that I'll never be able to stop running until Evgeny is stopped."

"I will stop him," Sebastian vowed. "I know that it's hard for you to trust me. But I'm telling you the truth."

"I know," she assured him. "And I wouldn't be here—I wouldn't risk leaving my child without a mother if I didn't trust you to protect me."

He sucked in a breath of surprise. "I hadn't realized that you did…" And now he had even more pressure to not let her down.

NOT ONLY DID SHE TRUST HIM—but she was also beginning to fall in love with him. But maybe neither of those was a burden he wanted. He already had a country depending on him; the last thing he needed was more responsibility.

"Maybe we should just give this up," she said as she hastily stepped back from him.

"Do you think Evgeny will give up?"

"No."

"Then neither will we," he said.

No matter how much responsibility he had, he was willing to take on more. To take on hers. "I can't thank you enough…for risking your life for me."

But she wanted to try to thank him. So she turned back around and slid her palms up his chest, and she stretched up his body and pressed her lips to his. He lowered his head and kissed her back, his mouth hungrily devouring hers. His tongue slid through her lips and tangled with hers.

Her skin heated and tingled as passion overwhelmed her. She trembled from the force of it.

With a deep groan, he pulled back. "I'm sorry…"

Now the heat of embarrassment rushed to her face. She had been so careful to avoid looking at him the past couple of days so that he would not notice how much she wanted him. But he was so damn handsome and chivalrous. "No. I'm sorry," she said. "You're here to protect. I know that's the only reason."

She forced a self-depreciating laugh. "I'm hardly your type." She glanced down at herself. The faded jeans and T-shirt had been washed so many times the seams were worn out.

Instead of the hot denial her ego needed, he hesitated a moment before chuckling. "I will admit that I have never dated anyone like you before."

"Who do you usually date?"

"Princesses. Heiresses," he replied.

She remembered that he'd told her his grandfather would have only approved of royalty. He would have hated her probably almost as much as he'd hated Sebastian's father. "I'm no heiress or princess."

"That's not what Samantha thinks," he reminded her of her daughter's sleepy proclamation the night she'd awakened to catch them kissing.

"She believes in fairy tales. I know better," Jessica said as disappointment clutched her heart. "In the real world, Cinderella would never get the prince."

"So you see yourself as Cinderella?"

She gestured down at her clothes. "Don't you?"

"You know what I see when I look at you?" he asked, fixing her with that implacable stare of his. "Not your clothes or your hair color. I see your spirit."

"What spirit?" she asked. Evgeny had beaten it out of her years ago, if she'd ever had much to begin with.

She'd never been strong and brave like Sam. She'd preferred to bury herself in a book and try to hide from the reality of their hand-to-mouth existence.

"The spirit that had you nearly dragging me behind your SUV when we first met," he reminded her with a grin of admiration. "Then had you shoving a shotgun in my face."

She had actually done that to a prince. She laughed, then sobered when she remembered why she'd done those things. "I was scared and desperate."

"Your spirit is what brought you here," he said. "You're scared but you wouldn't let a female deputy fill in for you. I've never dated anyone like you because I've never dated anyone as strong and brave and so damn sexy that every time I get close to you I struggle for control."

Her heart shifted, kicking against her ribs in reaction to his sweet words. No one had ever said such wonderful things to her. She launched herself at him, throwing her arms around his neck.

"It's that loss of control that I apologized for," he said, his muscular body full of tension. "After what you've been through, you need gentleness—tenderness—and I want you too much to be gentle."

She stretched up his body and bit his bottom lip. "I don't want gentleness. I just want you."

When he reached for her, she didn't flinch or cower. Instead she lifted her legs and wrapped them around his lean waist as he carried her up the stairs. His shoulders banged against the door and then the jamb as he entered her room. With its pale gray walls and lavender curtains and bedding, it had always been a stress-free oasis for her—more so because a man had never stepped inside it than because of its feminine decor. After the violence of her relationship with Evgeny, she had never wanted another man.

Until now.

With passion pumping hot and heavy in her blood, she clawed at Sebastian's shirt, tearing open its buttons to bare his muscular chest. Golden brown hair dusted golden skin. She skimmed her palms over his chest and abs to the buckle of his belt.

He rasped out a breath. "Slow down," he cautioned her, unwrapping her legs from around his waist so that she slid down his body. His erection strained against the fly of his jeans.

He wanted her, too. Feminine power filled her, but she stepped back from him. And instead of reaching for him again, she opened her blouse, fumbling every button free of the hole until the cotton parted and she could shrug off the shirt. Her bra was lace, so old and thin that her nipples shone through.

He groaned but didn't protest when she undid her own belt and unzipped her jeans. She paused a moment before pushing them down. While he stared so intently at her, she was worried about disappointing him. She had stretch marks and her hips had spread after having Samantha. She definitely couldn't compete with princesses or heiresses. But for him, she wanted to.

So she eased the jeans over her hips and kicked them off until she stood before him in just her underwear and boots. Then she removed those, too, and stood before him naked. But she'd been naked before him already, when she'd told him about her past.

And he'd been naked before her when he'd told her about his. They'd already been intimate when they'd shared those painful memories.

He released a ragged breath. "You are so beautiful…."

And the way he stared at her made her feel beautiful. Then he dropped his jeans. And she realized what true beauty was. Lean hips and long legs and…

She licked her lips. Then he did the same, dipping his head and running his tongue across her lips. He made love to her mouth, sliding his tongue in and out of her lips, tasting her and leaving his own rich flavor on her tongue.

Heat pooled between her legs. Then his hand was there, stroking through the curls. And his other hand slid over her shoulder and collarbone to the slope of her breast. His mouth followed his hand, spreading kisses like caresses until his lips closed around her taut nipple.

She cried out at the exquisite sensation. Then he slid a finger into her, winding up a pressure inside her so intense that she almost cried out again—in pain. But the pressure eased as little ripples of pleasure came over her.

It wasn't enough, though. She wanted him—all of him—no matter how big and intimidating he looked. She closed her hand around him, stroking her palm up and down the length of the engorged flesh.

He grunted and groaned. And his control snapped. He lifted her to the bed and followed her down, his body covering hers. He was so big, so strong, but she knew he would not be brutal. Instead of thrusting inside her, he moved over her body. Kissing her lips, her neck and lavishing attention on her breasts. She writhed against the sheets as the pressure built in intensity. She needed more.

And he gave it with his mouth, sliding his tongue where his finger had gone, stroking her to insanity. When she climaxed, she cried out his name, and he answered her plea, thrusting inside her, bringing her up again. Each thrust brought her closer to an ecstasy she'd never thought possible until it crashed over her and shattered her world.

He tensed and groaned and panted as if unable to catch his breath. Sweat beaded on his forehead and upper lip and then he thrust one last time. Deep. And filled her.

With a love she hadn't thought possible. She wrapped her arms around him and held him close for however long they had. Because forever wasn't possible—not with a prince.

"YOU'RE SURE BRENNER and those other men are out there?" Sebastian asked, the untraceable cell phone pressed to his ear. He divided his attention between the window, which was dark now as night had fallen, and the bed in which Jessica lay sleeping.

"I've been checking in with them almost as much as you and Jessica have been checking on me and Samantha."

"Is everything all right with her?"

"Great. I think I'll give up coruling and become a nanny." Beneath the sarcasm, there was affection. Just as quickly as Sebastian had, Antoine had fallen for the little girl. But Sebastian hadn't fallen just for Samantha; he'd fallen for Samantha's mother, too.

"I'm sorry this is taking so long," he apologized to his impatient brother. "I thought Evgeny would come after her right away."

"You think he's changed his mind?"

"No." Sebastian understood the man's obsession with her now. "He'll never let her go."

"Then why's he waiting?"

"He's playing with her," Sebastian said, "like a cat plays with a mouse, stalking and waiting." Messing with her head, building her fear of him. The man was more than a narcissist; he was a sadist, too.

"The guards have not seen anyone at all around the ranch. They haven't even noticed you."

Because he'd known that Evgeny was probably out there, watching, too, Sebastian had been careful to stay out of sight.

"Then he will come," he assured his twin. "He won't be able to resist."

Just as Sebastian hadn't been able to resist falling for Jessica—so hard and so deep that he couldn't bear the thought of her getting hurt. "I need to get a deputy out here to stand in for Jessica."

He could not bear the thought of her in danger, or worse yet, in the clutches of her ruthless husband.

"Jessica insisted on going with you," Antoine reminded him. "She said it wouldn't work otherwise."

"You're right that this was a crazy plan," Sebastian conceded. "I can't risk her life."

"The guards are out there," Antoine assured him. "Brenner can be trusted. He has your back."

"But still, I have to let him get close to her."

"Do you?" Antoine asked.

"Yes, close enough to threaten her." Or they wouldn't have grounds for the man's arrest.

"But isn't your real plan to shoot him before he gets close?" Antoine asked.

"What do you mean? The plan is to get him to come after and threaten her, so she can press charges."

"I know that's what you said, but I know you," Antoine said. "I know you don't plan to let that jerk get close to her ever again."

"I don't, but that doesn't mean I plan on killing him."

"You're going to have to," Antoine said. "I've checked this guy out. Killing him is the only way to stop him from killing you and her."

Chapter Fourteen

Sunlight, so bright that her lids glowed even before she opened them, warmed her face. She squinted against the glare and turned on her side. Then she blinked again in disbelief.

He was too handsome to be real. And even naked, he was regal—all arrogant planes of hard muscle rippling under silky-smooth skin. She would have thought last night was a dream if he wasn't lying beside her. But even as close as he was, he was out of her reach.

And as soon as he found his friend and who was behind the attack on the royals, he'd go back to his country. He had greater obligations than keeping her safe. A sense of foreboding had the skin prickling on her nape and her stomach muscles tightening; she didn't feel safe anymore. But the danger came more from the man lying beside her than the one from her past.

He would hurt her, too. Not physically. But he would hurt her emotionally because he could never return her feelings. Even though his grandfather was dead, it was obvious he wanted the approval the king had denied him. So he wouldn't make the mistake he'd felt his mother had made; he wouldn't marry a commoner.

Only royalty.

She would never be a princess.

Being careful to not disturb him, she eased out of bed and quickly dressed. But when she turned back, his eyes were open, and he watched her with that intent stare of his. "Where are you going?"

"I have to feed the animals," she reminded him.

"I hate your going out to the barn by yourself."

"Those guards would have warned you if anyone had tried coming onto the ranch." A man named Brenner kept calling and checking in, assuring him that no one had tried breaching the perimeter.

"True," he said, tossing back the blankets. Fortunately he'd pulled his boxers on sometime during the night, but the black silk rode low on his lean hips, tempting her to reach out and push them down.

Desire heated her blood and her skin, and she wanted nothing more than to run her hands and lips over him as she had again and again in the night. But the day had come and with it reality. Last night had only been a dream, a fairy tale that would never come true.

She turned away from him and the temptation he presented, and headed toward the door. But he caught her wrist and tugged her back.

"So because the guards haven't forewarned us of anyone trying to get onto the ranch, it's safe for me to take care of the animals. I'll just stick to the shadows, so no one notices me heading toward the barn."

"What shadows?" She glanced toward the window, but the light was almost all gone now, dark clouds having blocked out the sun. "Still, it's not part of the plan…"

"I need to get out of the house for a minute," he admitted. "Get some air."

She wasn't the only one having regrets about their night of make-believe. No one knew better than he did that they had no future. "But you don't know what to feed the animals," she pointed out.

"You wrote out the directions when we were waiting at the hospital with Helen in case someone else had to feed the animals while she recovered."

Because she hadn't planned to come back here. She'd intended instead to take her daughter and run. She should have done that.

But Sebastian had gotten to her with his words about her not letting go of Evgeny. She had been carrying the man inside her head even as she'd run from him. So she'd known that no matter how far she ran, she would never get away from him…unless she could stop him from following her. For good.

But unless she killed him, she would never get rid of Evgeny for good. Prison hadn't held him the first time; she doubted it could hold him a second.

"You took the directions?" she asked.

"I remember what you wrote down," he replied. "I'll

call and check in with the security team before I leave you alone in the house. Then I'll sneak out to the barn."

Maybe she wasn't the only one who wanted to run away. She nodded in agreement, no matter which one of them went out to the barn, she would have some badly needed time alone. And when Sebastian came back inside, she'd be packed and ready to leave.

She was running. And not just from Evgeny...

SEBASTIAN KEPT TO THE SHADOWS as he moved from the house to the barn. He'd just checked in with Brenner for an update on the perimeter. No one had tried to breach it yet. Perhaps Evgeny wasn't waiting to get Jessica alone; perhaps he was waiting for her to leave. Then he would grab her on some deserted stretch of road.

And Jessica would never be seen again. Perhaps the man wouldn't take her life but he would take her spirit, and that would kill her just as effectively. Sebastian could not let that happen.

He pulled open the door to the barn. Heat radiated from the dark interior, along with the odor of hay and other less aromatic scents. They had barns at the palace in Barajas. And ever since they'd gone to live there, if Sebastian needed to find Antoine, the barns were usually where he searched first. He would find him with the horses or the other livestock: cows and goats and sheep. When they had taken over as corulers, Antoine kept building more barns and fencing more pastures.

He would have loved this ranch. Sebastian just wanted to get the animals fed, so he could return to Jessica. He wanted to wrap his arms around her and hold her close. But she hadn't wanted that this morning. She'd wanted space. Hell, after last night, so had he.

He had never felt as deep a connection to any other human being—not even his twin—as he had to her. They hadn't just made love; they'd become one. One heart. One soul.

Feelings had overwhelmed him. And perhaps he had overwhelmed Jessica. As she had complained, he was too arrogant, too autocratic. King Omar had trained him and Antoine to be the rulers she'd accused him of being. Ruthless. After his years in the military, ruthlessness came too easily to him.

Tenderness and gentleness did not. He was not the man she needed. After all she'd been through, she deserved someone as sweet and sensitive as she was.

The animals shifted restlessly in their stalls, drawing his attention back to his task. He'd watched Jessica write out the directions, but that had been a couple of days ago. He didn't remember exact measurements of the feed, so he just filled the bowls. The animals remained restless though, the horses skittish while the cats hid in the loft.

His stomach muscles clenched, his gut sending him a warning. Too late. Because it wasn't cats he'd heard in the loft. Nor was it a cat that jumped from the loft onto his back, knocking him to the ground.

It was a burly man whose heavily muscled arm encircled Sebastian's neck, cutting off his breath while straining the bones. He hadn't used hand-to-hand combat in the military, but he'd learned it. He knew how to break someone's neck, and apparently so did this man.

That military training had been long ago, but he called on it now—not to save himself but to save Jessica. Once he was no longer a threat, they would go after her. He slammed his elbow into the guy's side, then bucked him off. Before the guy could roll to his feet, Sebastian was on top of him, throwing punches. The man's face was already deeply gouged, but now blood spurted from his nose and lip. Still, he managed to get his hands around Sebastian's throat.

The guy's grip tightened, threatening to squeeze off Sebastian's airway. His lungs burning for air, Sebastian pulled the guy's hands from his neck and lurched back. But before he could get to his feet, something struck the back of his head and shoulders, knocking him to the ground again.

Dirt and straw burned his eyes while pain radiated throughout him. A foot kicked his side, the pointed toe of the boot striking his ribs. Ignoring the excruciating pain of a cracking bone, he grabbed the guy's leg and pulled him off his feet.

The guy grunted when his head struck the ground. The gun he had used to hit Sebastian over the back of the head flew across the barn floor, picking up dirt and straw as it skittered away. Sebastian dived for it, but the other guy, still bleeding, swore and launched himself at it, too.

Sebastian caught him with his elbow again against the guy's jaw. But the man did not let go, pummeling Sebastian's sides with his fists. He stretched, trying to reach for the weapon. But it was too far.

So he used other weapons. His fists, elbows and knees until the guy rolled off him and onto the floor, groaning in pain. Groaning himself, he lurched to his feet and reached for the weapon, but another gun cocked.

He looked to the guy who'd struck him with the gun, but he still lay on the floorboards. So he turned toward the barn door and the blond-haired man who stepped from the shadows. His eyes glinted as coldly as the Glock he held, the barrel pointed directly at Sebastian.

"How did you get onto the ranch?" he asked. "What did you do to my men?"

"Nothing," Evgeny replied with that smirk that made Sebastian want to smash his fist into his face. "They were eager to betray you."

Sebastian shook his head. Antoine had vetted the men; they would not have turned easily. Not without a lot of incentive. "No."

"Don't feel too badly," Evgeny said. "I was wrong about my men, too." The men in question lurched to their feet, the one who'd lost his weapon quickly retrieving it. "They are much weaker than I thought—for a pampered prince to have been able to overpower them."

"Put down the guns," Sebastian challenged, "and I'll show you how pampered I am. Just you and me. Man to man." He hated Jessica's ex enough to kill him with his bare hands.

Evgeny chuckled. "I am tempted. It would not take me long to show you how a real man fights. But I have already kept my sweet Teresa waiting too long for me. I would rather show her a real man."

Heedless of the guns, Sebastian jumped forward but the first man kicked his legs out, knocking him to the ground. Then, as if to prove to his boss that he was not weak, he struck Sebastian repeatedly with his fists. Blood trickled into his mouth, but that was not what he tasted. He tasted fear—not for his life but for Jessica's. He never should have allowed her back onto the ranch. This was all his fault.

Rage filled him. Like his father, he would not go down without a fight. He swung out, dropping Evgeny's man with one fist to the jaw. Then he vaulted to his feet and launched himself at the boss.

But before he could get close to Evgeny, a shot rang out. He dropped to the ground, more from instinct than because he'd been hit. Hell, he was in so much pain from the beatings that he wasn't certain if he had been hit.

A GASP SLIPPED THROUGH Jessica's lips. She didn't believe she had hit anyone, but then she'd never fired a gun like the one Sebastian had brought to the ranch. She'd fired into the loft, but maybe Evgeny had fired, too.

And hit Sebastian. He lay on the ground, unmoving, blood trickling from the corner of his mouth over his stubborn chin. Fear and pain clutched her heart. She needed to go to him, needed to help him.

But she wouldn't be helping him if she moved. The only movement she could make was shoving the barrel of the gun between Evgeny's shoulders blades. "The next shot will go right through you," she warned him, "taking out your heart, if you actually had one."

"You know I have one," he said, his body tense. But his eyes, his evil eyes, must have directed his men because they moved toward Sebastian, dragging him to his feet.

Blood spattered his chambray shirt and jeans but didn't saturate the cloth. He had no gunshot wound, just swelling and bruising. But no matter how hurt he was, his concern was all for her. Because while Evgeny's men held him, they had weapons pointed at her.

"You know I love you," Evgeny continued. "I have always loved you."

"Prove it," she challenged him. "Let me go."

"I can't do that."

"Then let him go," she urged.

"I can't do that, either," Evgeny said, feigning regret as he had so many other emotions since she'd known him. "He tried to take you from me. I can't let him live."

She forced a chuckle. "He doesn't want anything to

do with me but to protect me. Just like Sam, he has that overdeveloped sense of responsibility."

"That overdeveloped sense of responsibility got your brother killed," Evgeny replied.

Skin prickled on her nape. Was there more to her brother's murder than Evgeny had told her? "What about Sam?"

He tensed even more but shook his head. "We're talking about the prince now. Cavanaugh here doesn't just want to protect you," Evgeny continued. "And you know it."

She forced another laugh. "You think he wants me? A married woman with a child? He only wants the information I can give him about his missing friend."

"Then he's talking to the wrong person," Evgeny said. "I can tell him more than you can."

"You know where Amir is?" Sebastian asked.

"Better yet, I know who's after you." He laughed. "I know who's after all of you."

Sebastian snorted, probably calling the Russian's bluff. "No, you don't."

"Of course I do. I rule a much larger world than you do. I have connections you will never have. That is truly how I found Teresa. A former associate of mine, here on business, recognized her from the picture I have hanging in my office."

He glanced over his shoulder at her. "Our wedding picture. He said you'd changed your appearance, though, so he wasn't entirely sure it was you. That was why I sent Dmitri and Nic ahead to seek you out."

He nodded at Sebastian. "And when you held that little press conference of yours, you made that easy for them, just like you and your friends are making it easy for your enemy to kill you."

"What enemy?" Sebastian asked.

"It doesn't matter now," Evgeny said, "because you've made a far more dangerous enemy in me."

Jessica nudged the barrel deeper into Evgeny's back. "Tell him who is trying to kill him and the others."

He glanced over his shoulder again. His eyes cold and hard, her husband warned her, "You know that I do not like being told what to do."

"If you don't do what I tell you, I will shoot you," she threatened.

"And then my men will shoot your white knight."

The guy who'd grabbed her a few days ago pressed the barrel of his gun against Sebastian's temple.

"And after they shoot him, they'll shoot you," Evgeny promised.

"You intend to kill us anyway," she said. "At least this way you'll die, too."

"I do not want you dead," he said. "I just want you. I want my wife and my child. I want my *family*."

"She isn't here." And she had never been so thankful to be separated from her baby.

"She's with his brother," Evgeny said. "For now. Soon she will be with me."

This was why she had always feared him. There was nothing he didn't know.

"You won't get to Samantha," Sebastian said, his blue gaze promising Jessica that her daughter was safe.

"After your friend Brenner talked to you, he called Prince Antoine. You think he's still at the resort when he knows his brother is about to be killed?" Evgeny shook his head. "You know him better than that."

He was right. Antoine would definitely come to his brother's aid. After their parents' brutal murders, they were all each other had.

And Samantha was all Jessica had.

"When he rushes away from the resort, he will leave Samantha with someone who will bring her right to her loving daddy," Evgeny gloated.

"You're just giving me another reason to shoot you," Jessica warned him. She needed to pull the trigger, her finger twitched against it. But Evgeny wasn't lying; his men would do as he'd told them. And she and Sebastian would die, too.

"I just want my family," Evgeny said. "That's all I want."

"Then let Prince Cavanaugh go," she urged him again. "If you let him leave here, unharmed, I'll go with you." Especially since someone was bringing Samantha to him.

Evgeny chuckled. "But if I hold on to him, I could get his brother to pay a handsome ransom for him."

"But you don't want money," she reminded him.

"Since taking over your father's enterprises, you have more than enough of that anyways."

Evgeny grinned. "Probably more money than your prince here, since he's in America to beg for trade agreements—to beg for money from our government."

"Yes, that's why he's here," Jessica reminded him. "Just for business. Not for me. He'll go back to his island nation and leave me alone."

"I will never leave you alone," Evgeny said, making the same promise he had at Sam's funeral. Then, his vow had touched her heart; now, it chilled it because she knew he spoke the truth.

"You said you want me," she continued, choking on the bile that rose in her throat at the horrible thought of being his wife again. "Let me be Prince Sebastian's ransom. I'll leave with you, and I will never run away from you again."

Evgeny turned his head so that he could meet her gaze over his shoulder. Hope warmed his usually cold gray eyes. "Really?"

"I'll be your wife," she promised. "Samantha and I will be your family. Just don't hurt Sebastian." Any more than his men already had.

"Then put down the gun," Evgeny said.

"Don't do it," Sebastian warned her, his blue gaze intense. The guy pressed the gun harder against his head, cocking his neck at a painful angle.

Ignoring the prince, she asked her husband, "Do I have your promise?"

"If you promise to never run away again," Evgeny negotiated.

"I swear," she vowed. "As long as he lives, I'll live with you."

Sebastian cursed. "Don't…"

"Then we have a deal," Evgeny said, nodding toward his men who pulled the barrel away from Sebastian's head. "Drop the gun, Teresa."

"Don't do it," Sebastian pleaded. "Just shoot him."

Jessica shook her head, unable to pull the trigger. "This doesn't concern you," she told him. "This is between me and my husband." Then, her hands shaking, she dropped the gun.

The barrel no longer pressing into his back, Evgeny whirled around toward her. Using his gun, he struck her across the face, knocking her to the ground.

Pain exploded in her head, momentarily blinding her. But she blinked back the tears burning in her eyes and focused on Sebastian. The men held him back as Evgeny, his hand tangled in her hair, dragged her to her feet.

"You, wife, don't tell me what to do," he said. "You will never leave me…because I will never let you."

He turned back to his men and ordered, "Kill him."

Chapter Fifteen

Fighting not just for his life but hers, Sebastian swung his arm, knocking the gun from the hand of the man who'd had it pressed against his temple. A blast went off, sending the animals into a frenzy. They kicked the sides of their stalls, whinnied and neighed.

But the real animal was Evgeny. His hand still fisted in Jessica's hair, he dragged her toward the open barn door. But she wrestled against his grasp, kicking out, kicking the long rifle toward Sebastian. He grabbed it up, but before he could focus and fire it, Evgeny squeezed off some shots, not caring if he hit Sebastian or his own men.

Sebastian rolled across the floor, taking cover behind some stacked bales of hay as bullets ricocheted around the barn.

"The next shot is going straight into her head," Evgeny warned.

Jessica screamed out, more desperation than pain in her voice. "Don't let him get Samantha. Please…"

"She's safe," he assured her.

He had made Antoine promise that no matter what the situation he would not leave the little girl alone. Antoine would never go back on his word.

Neither would Sebastian. He had vowed to protect Jessica; he would not fail. But when he edged from behind the hay, more shots rang out. Not from Evgeny's gun but from the man Sebastian had not disarmed. He covered his boss while Evgeny dragged Jessica toward a car parked behind the Suburban. The tires of the rusted SUV had been slashed, leaving him no way to pursue them.

Especially if his security team had been compromised or killed. Antoine could not have been wrong about Brenner and the other men. Brenner had sounded strange when Sebastian had called him earlier; he'd been coerced into saying that all was clear.

How had Sebastian failed so badly in his surveillance that he hadn't even noticed their approach to the ranch? Because he'd been making love with Jessica instead of protecting her.

He had already broken his promise to her.

He leaned out farther, but gunfire drove him back. The other man had retrieved his weapon. They were both shooting at him. But Sebastian had to keep his gaze on Jessica; he could not let her out of his sight.

The car engine revved as Evgeny threw it into reverse, backing up to the barn before slamming the transmission into Drive and heading toward the road. Just as she'd feared, her husband had come for her. And while Sebastian hunkered down behind bales of hay, the car was getting farther and farther away.

JESSICA HAD KNOWN that Evgeny wouldn't keep his promise. But she hadn't known how else to buy herself and Sebastian some time. The prince had given her a chance to take back her life; she'd had to do the same for him. Despite his brother's call to the ranch warning her that the perimeter guards had been compromised, she hadn't obeyed his order to hide. She'd known that he wouldn't be able to get help to his brother before Evgeny killed him.

Only she could save Sebastian. So she'd grabbed up his gun and headed out to the barn.

Evgeny laughed. "How does that man rule a country? He is weak and stupid. I can't believe you trusted him to protect you."

She trusted Sebastian. To protect Samantha. It was too late for her. She had to protect herself now, as she should have years ago. "Sebastian is honorable. He keeps his word, unlike you. You promised you'd let him go."

"You think you are a worthy ransom for a prince?" He laughed. "There is a far bigger price on his head than your life."

"Who?" she asked. "Who put the hit out on him and the other royals?"

He laughed. "Why do you want to know? You will

never speak to him again. I am sure he is already dead."

She gasped as pain clutched her heart. She couldn't imagine a world without Sebastian in it, even if he was a world away on his island nation.

"That is what happens to anyone who tries to come between us," Evgeny continued. "Your brother had to learn that, too."

"Sam?"

"He knew I was going to propose to you. He didn't think I was good enough for his sweet sister." Bitterness twisted Evgeny's face into a grotesque mask of evil. "He was going to try to keep you away from me, just like the prince tried."

"You killed Sam?"

He sighed. "I hated to do it, but I wasn't going to lose you. Then or now."

"But he was your friend."

"So?" he scoffed. "I turned on my father, too, for you. When you served me with those divorce papers, I had to get out of prison. I knew the only way out was to offer the Feds what they wanted most."

"Your own father?"

"You'd begged me to do it for years," he reminded her, "because of how he'd hurt me. You loved me, and you didn't want me to become what my father was."

That was why she had opened the door to him that night—the night he'd put her in the hospital and gotten her pregnant with Jessica. Because she'd believed that he might have finally become the man she'd thought he could be. She had believed he'd turned in his father because he'd wanted to be a better man. For her.

Just like Samantha, she used to believe in fairy tales. But that night had proved to her once and for all that they never came true.

"Your father deserved to be behind bars," she said, "because he is an evil man." But his son was even more of a monster than he was.

Uncaring of the gun he pointed at her, the gun that already had her face swelling, she grabbed for the steering wheel. She didn't care about herself; she only cared that Evgeny finally be stopped.

"STOP!" THE PRINCE SHOUTED from behind the bale of hay into which Dmitri had emptied his clip.

Had he been hit? The driver had—his shoulder bled as he slumped against one of the barn walls, and was either losing consciousness or dying. The boss had hit him when he'd fired into the barn on his way out, leaving them behind with no transportation.

"You will not escape," Prince Sebastian said, as if he'd read Dmitri's mind. "My brother will have sent other men out here. They will be here soon. That's why your boss took off before making sure I was dead. So put down your weapon."

The prince was right. There was no way out. If Dmitri was apprehended, he would be sent to prison for the rest of his life, however long that lasted. Did Wyoming have the death penalty? He had killed the men who'd guarded the perimeter of the ranch; they hadn't turned as Evgeny had claimed. They'd been loyal to the prince. And look what their loyalty had earned them.

Death.

The same as Dmitri's loyalty to his boss would earn him. But if he was going to die, he would at least die with honor—carrying out the last of his orders.

To kill the prince.

He slid in a new clip. Then, his gun gripped tightly in his hand, he charged the hay bales, firing shot after shot at the prince. Dmitri would die today. But he would not die alone...

SEBASTIAN SPARED ONLY a glance to the man dying at his feet before heading toward the ladder that led up to the loft. Another gun cocked, but when he swung back to fire at the other shooter, the man had already lost the weapon as it slipped from his grasp. And the life slipped from his eyes.

Sliding the strap on the gun over his shoulder, Sebastian climbed into the loft and jumped over more bales of hay to reach the small window in the peak of the roof. He pushed the little shutter door open and slid his gun out, bracing the barrel on the jamb.

Pushing all his fear, anger and regret from his mind, he focused on the scope, staring through it to track the car. It swerved across the driveway as two people struggled for control of the steering wheel. Evgeny might have beaten her again, but he had not destroyed her spirit.

She was still the strong, brave woman with whom Sebastian had fallen so deeply in love. He should have told her—should have given her the words he'd never spoken to anyone else. He might not have the chance to declare his feelings if the car didn't stop careening back and forth.

She was not making his shot easy.

You are just like your father. More liability than responsibility. Just like him, you will fail when it matters most...

His grandfather's hateful words echoed in his mind as they had ever since the bitter old man had uttered them. Sebastian had tried to shake off the taunts as easily as Antoine had, but he could not forget that Omar had been right about their father.

But he had to be wrong about Sebastian. Because this moment was when it mattered most that he not fail. For through the scope, he could see clearly inside the car. While Jessica fought for the steering wheel, Evgeny only held it with one hand while he lifted his gun with the other and pointed it to her beautiful face.

Sebastian fought down his panic over losing her. He fought down his doubts. He stopped breathing, even stopped his heart from beating, as he centered the crosshairs of the scope on the back of a blond head. He prayed the car stopped swerving for a moment. Just a moment was all he needed. Careful not to breathe or move anything but his finger on the trigger, Sebastian took the shot.

But the car veered. Violently. It swerved off the driveway and landed, spinning tires up, into the steep ditch between the gravel drive and the pasture.

He refocused the scope to see inside the car through the back window. Blood spattered the broken windshield—on both the driver and passenger sides. And two heads were pinned between the roof and the dashboard.

Instead of saving the woman he loved, had he killed her?

Chapter Sixteen

Sirens wailed in the distance as the help they'd needed finally approached. Too late.

Sebastian panted for breath, his lungs burning as he ran down the driveway. Finally he neared the site of the crash and scrambled down the steep slope of the ditch. Weeds and briars caught at his clothes as if trying to hold him back from what he feared he would see.

Horrific images from his childhood flitted through his mind. All that blood, just like the blood that ran over the shattered glass of the broken windshield now. Evgeny was dead. He only had to glance at the Russian to know the man had died as violently as he'd lived. He would never be able to hurt Jessica again.

But how hurt was she? Had Evgeny taken his shot, too, before Sebastian had terminated him? Pain and panic clutched at his heart as he considered that nightmare—the one of finding the woman he loved dead.

His lungs burning now with fear, Sebastian pushed through the weeds to the passenger's side of the crumpled, upside-down car. His hands shaking, he grabbed the door handle and pulled. The metal refused to yield. Jessica was still held captive alongside the man who'd terrorized her. Giving up on the door, Sebastian pulled the shattered glass from the passenger window and wedged himself through the narrow opening to reach for her.

Her blood trickled over his fingers as he pushed her hair back and felt for a pulse in her neck. It pounded fast and hard beneath his fingers.

His heart swelled with hope. She was alive. For now. "Jessica?"

She moaned and shifted against the seat that was now on top of her. Sebastian gripped her shoulder and the back of her head. "Don't move, sweetheart. You could be seriously injured."

Even if Evgeny hadn't shot her, the crash could have broken her neck. Because she hadn't been wearing a seat belt, she'd rolled with the car and was now pinned between the dashboard and the seat. He lifted his head to look for the emergency vehicles. Lights flashed as they pulled off the main road and headed down the drive to the ranch.

"Help will be here soon," he promised. "Sit tight."

It would take the jaws of life to extract her battered body from the vehicle.

Ignoring his order and his concern, she moved again and turned slightly toward the driver's side. A gasp of shock slipped through her lips. "He's dead…"

"I know."

"You shouldn't have killed him," she murmured.

Regret clutched his heart. Had Evgeny been right? Had she still cared about him even after everything he'd done to her? Had they had some connection that Sebastian would never understand? That he would never have with her…

"I shouldn't have," he agreed, "because you got hurt." But if he hadn't killed him and Evgeny had pulled the trigger…

The tires of the sheriff's white Dodge SUV squealed as it braked on the drive. "Help is here. You'll be all right. Everything will be all right."

"No," Jessica murmured. "Not now that he's dead…"

"If he'd lived, you would have never been safe," he reminded her.

Perhaps Antoine had been right—that Sebastian had intended to kill him all along even though he hadn't consciously admitted it to himself. But deep down he'd known that the only way to stop a man like Evgeny was with a bullet.

"But if he'd lived, he could have told you who was behind the explosion," she said. "He knew who is after you and the other royals. Someone is determined that all of you be killed."

He'd nearly forgotten about the danger he and the others were in because he'd been so focused on Jessica since meeting her. Even though Evgeny was dead, she wasn't safe if she stayed anywhere near Sebastian.

ISOLATED BEHIND THE white curtain separating her cubicle from the rest of the ones in the emergency room, Jessica had never felt so alone. Not even when Sam had died—murdered by his best friend. By the man she'd been fool enough to marry.

And now she'd done it again; she'd fallen for the wrong man. Just as she'd suspected Sebastian had only been concerned for her safety. It was that overdeveloped sense of responsibility that made him ideal for ruling a nation. He'd acted out of protectiveness, not love, when he'd risked his life for hers.

And now that she was no longer in danger, he was gone. She'd ridden alone in the ambulance from the ranch to the hospital. She hadn't asked him to ride along, though. She'd asked him to bring Samantha to her instead.

"Where's my mommy?" a soft voice fearfully whispered.

"I'm here," Jessica replied, pulling back the curtain.

Her little girl was clasped tight in the arms of a prince, whose blue-eyed gaze studied her. But Antoine did not look at her as Sebastian did. He could not see inside her. Instead his gaze skimmed across her face.

She lifted a hand to the painful bruise. Maybe she shouldn't have had Samantha brought to her.

"I'm okay," she assured her baby, who stared at her with eyes that same steely gray as her father's.

Jessica's last image of Evgeny was of those eyes, open but blind in death. She shuddered.

"You're okay?" Samantha asked.

"Yes." She held out her arms. "I just need a hug, sweetheart." She just needed her child; that was all she'd ever needed. She did not need Sebastian Cavanaugh, so she shoved aside her hurt feelings that he had not brought her daughter to her.

And she smiled up at his brother. "Thank you, Prince Antoine...so much."

"Sebastian made me promise to not let her out of my sight," Antoine explained, "that yours were the only arms into which I would release her."

And even though he'd feared for his brother's life, he had kept his promise. She could not imagine how emotionally torn he must have been, and his stern face gave away nothing of his struggle. But because she knew Sebastian so well, she felt as if she knew Antoine, too. Wishing she could say more, she just reiterated, "Thank you..."

Samantha leaned forward and gently pressed her lips to Jessica's swollen cheek. "There, Mommy, does that feel better?"

She blinked back tears of pain at even that slight pressure against her wound. "Yes, sweetheart, I'm all better."

"What happened?" The little girl's bottom lip quivered as her eyes flooded with tears. "Did the bad men that hurt Helen come after you?"

"No," she lied. "I was in an accident." She tightened her arms around her baby. "So were the bad men. They're all gone now. They can't hurt Helen, or me, or you, or anyone else. We're safe, baby."

She released a shuddery breath of relief. All those years of living in fear that he would find her were finally over.

"We're safe," she repeated.

SEBASTIAN TURNED AWAY, unable to intrude on the emotional reunion of mother and daughter—unable to intrude with the reality that she wasn't safe. Not yet.

But Antoine had noticed him, and he had no such qualms as he joined Sebastian in the waiting room. "If you don't tell her, I will."

Sebastian turned toward his twin, fixing him under the stare he used like a weapon.

Antoine just shook his head. "You can't let her believe she's safe when we both know that she's not. She was right about her ex being behind these threats on her life. But there will be more threats."

"She didn't witness anything that can lead us to who was behind the explosion," Sebastian reminded him. "Hell, we still don't have a clue where Amir is."

"At least we learned that he definitely survived the explosion."

"But we don't know if he's still alive." Sebastian groaned. "If he was, wouldn't he have contacted us by now?"

Antoine shrugged. "Perhaps he does not know who he can trust."

"He can trust us. We're targets just as much as he is." And that was why he had to let Jessica go, because it was not safe for her to be around him. Back at the ranch, the sheriff and Jane Cameron had informed him that the bullet from the armrest in his Hummer was of a different caliber than the guns Evgeny and his men had carried. There had been someone else out in the Badlands that day trying to kill him.

"That bomb was intended for all us," Sebastian reminded his twin. "How could Amir think that one of us might be behind it?"

Antoine shrugged. "We don't know what he is thinking. Hell, I am your twin and I don't know what *you're* thinking."

"What do you mean?"

"Are you just going to let that woman and child go?" he asked, his voice gruff with disgust.

"I will give her the reward," Sebastian said. "She will have enough money to start a new life."

"Will she and the child have a life if you let them out of your sight?"

"They stand a better chance at being safe away from me than with me," Sebastian explained. And for that reason and that reason alone, he had to let her go. "They won't get caught in the cross fire when someone tries to kill us. There are definitely orders out there to kill us. Her ex knew who had put out those orders."

"He did not tell her before he died?"

"No." And for that reason, for his sake only, she had regretted the man's death. Sebastian understood that now…because as she'd been extricated from the crash, she'd shared that Evgeny had confessed to killing her brother.

Sebastian did not regret killing him.

"But the person who put out the order, he will not know that," Antoine said.

"When no one comes after him, he'll realize she is no threat," Sebastian argued. "I will have to hide her for only a little while." Far away from himself.

"You don't know that," Antoine said. "This person will also know she is the witness. He will not know what she did or did not see. Or if she really doesn't know Amir's whereabouts. She could be abducted and tortured to reveal what she knows."

Sebastian gasped in pain and not from his injuries. He imagined instead what she might be subjected to—worse even than what Evgeny had done to her. He flinched. "That will not happen. I will make it known that she is no threat."

"She's not the threat," Antoine agreed. "You are."

Sebastian sucked in a breath.

"It's obvious how much you care about her. That makes her your weakness. She and Samantha could be kidnapped and held in exchange for your life." Like she had exchanged her life for his, except Evgeny had broken the agreement she'd made with him.

"Or they could be used as leverage to get you to withdraw from the trade agreement between COIN and the United States," Antoine continued. "That's probably why the hit is out on us—to stop the agreement from going through. You don't want Jessica and Samantha to be used against you."

That was why, at thirty-seven and despite the need for heirs, Sebastian had never married. He had not wanted to put a wife and children in the same danger their father had put them in because of his past. He suspected that Antoine had not married for that same reason.

"That's why I have to let them go—to protect them," he admitted, his throat thick with emotion. "I couldn't bear for them to get hurt because of me."

"You don't think you're hurting her right now?" Antoine asked. "I saw her face—"

"Evgeny struck her with the gun."

"I'm not talking about the swelling. I'm talking about that look of utter devastation on her face when she realized that it was me bringing Samantha to her and not you."

"I need to stay away from her," he said, trying to convince himself more than he was trying to convince his twin. "All of us royals are targets. I can't put her and Samantha at risk, too."

"So get them out of here."

"That's what I've been telling you I'm going to do," Sebastian reminded him, his temper fraying. "I'm going to get her to take that damn reward and get the hell out of here."

"You'll be able to let her go?"

Pain clutched his heart at the thought of watching her walk away from him. It would be nearly as hard as when Evgeny had dragged her away. "I would do anything for her and Samantha," he said. "Even let her go."

"They'd be safer with you than away from you."

He shook his head.

"You're not our father, no matter what our grandfather told you. You proved that today when you saved Jessica's life."

"It was close," he admitted, his voice cracking. "You saw her face." That blow haunted him, like the accident pinning her inside the blood-spattered car. "You were right that my plan was too dangerous. She could have died. I can't take that risk again."

"Then take her home."

"What?"

"Take her and Samantha back to Barajas with you. It would be easier to keep her safe there, surrounded by people we know we can trust."

"Can we?" Sebastian asked. "You don't think the king of Sarek is behind the explosion and attacks?" Sarek was close to Barajas, too close given its propensity for warfare, but it had declined to be part of COIN due to King Kalil Ramat's hatred of America.

"Rumor has it that he has used Russian hit men," Antoine recalled, "to suppress any challenges to his throne. You really think he could be behind everything?"

"I don't know. It could be anyone." If only Evgeny would have given him the name… "Like Dad, you and I made more than our share of enemies during our years of military service."

Antoine clenched his jaw and jerked his head in an abrupt nod. "True. But it's also true that you'd be able to keep Samantha and Jessica safest on Barajas, even with Sarek so close. You managed to protect them both here. It'll be far easier at home."

Their parents wouldn't have died had they all been living in the security of the palace. But because the king had not approved their marriage, they'd been living in Europe, in exile from both their lands. Perhaps that was why Grandfather had been so determined to blame their father, because it had been easier for him than acknowledging his own blame.

Sebastian nodded. "You're right."

"Of course I'm right," Antoine replied. "We've both been away too long anyway. It's time for one of us to go home."

"But I shouldn't leave you here—alone."

"I'm not alone. Stefan and Efraim are here, too. And I believe we can trust Sheriff Wolf. Working together, we'll find Amir soon. I know it."

"But you had my back." Always. "I should have yours."

"You have more important concerns than my safety," Antoine said.

"I have theirs." He glanced toward the doors to the emergency room. "She's stubborn and strong and independent. She may not agree to go with me."

Antoine shrugged. "She may not, but then I've never known you to take no for an answer. Or I would not have been playing nanny the past few days."

"She's even more stubborn than you are."

"True. When I lost contact with Brenner, I called the ranch and told her to hide and wait until I got help to you," Antoine shared. "But she didn't wait."

"No."

"She loves you. And I do not have to ask if you love her. You would not have been so willing to let her go if you did not love her."

"You know that love only complicates the situation."

"Grandfather is gone," Antoine said. "You should not be listening to him anymore. It is not because our father was not royalty that he and our mother were killed."

"No. It wasn't because of what Father wasn't but because of what he was."

Antoine shrugged. "You are not our father or our grandfather. You need to listen to your heart. Let it tell you what's best."

Sebastian wasn't convinced that letting her go wouldn't be the best thing to do. But he realized he loved her too much to do that. She had trusted him to protect her.

Would she trust him to love her? Could he convince a woman who'd lived the life she had to believe in fairy tales?

Chapter Seventeen

It's like a fairy tale.

As the plane neared the runway, the beauty of the island stole her breath. It was so lush and green with splashes of vibrant color in lakes and flowers. And the water surrounding it was so clear and blue and deep.

Like Sebastian's eyes…

She glanced over at him, but he was busy with Samantha, pointing out the window to show her his island. His…

Like she longed to be. But he had only invited her to his home because of his overdeveloped sense of responsibility. He and the other royals believed that she and Samantha were still in danger because the media had learned that she was the witness.

But she had witnessed nothing of any use to anyone. If only Evgeny had told her who was behind the attempts on their lives…

But Evgeny had never done anything to help her— only to hurt her. Yet Sebastian, who was only trying to help her, might hurt her far worse than Evgeny ever had. Because he was giving her false hope, making her believe that it might be possible for the fairy tale to come true.

She closed her eyes to all of it and murmured, "It's not real."

"What's not real, Mommy?" Samantha asked.

She forced a smile. "Nothing."

Everything. The private plane. The island. The prince. None of it felt real. She had to be back at the ranch, in her bed dreaming. Soon Helen's old rooster would crow and wake her at the crack of dawn. And she would discover that none of it had really happened. She hadn't witnessed an explosion. She hadn't met Sebastian after the press conference he'd held two weeks ago. She hadn't made love with him.

But if none of that had really happened, then Evgeny was still out there, searching for her...

She trembled at the horror that would be, living with the burden of all that fear again. A big hand covered hers, offering comfort and heat with just the squeeze of his long, sensual fingers.

She wanted to feel them on her skin again, caressing her as he had that night, a week ago. She lifted her gaze to his mouth. The swelling had gone down, his split lip healed. She wanted to kiss him. But he hadn't asked her to come home with him because he loved her. He'd asked her because he wanted to protect her, because he felt responsible for her safety.

"The pilot is very good," he assured her. "The landing will be smooth."

Just like every other assurance he had offered her, this one was warranted, too. They landed without incident. It was the disembarking that scared her. So many of his subjects had gathered at the airport, with flowers and signs to welcome their ruler home. The media was also present, but unlike the reporters in Dumont, these did not hurl impudent questions. Instead, like his other subjects, they just welcomed him back.

Everyone adored him. His subjects. Samantha. And most of all, her. She loved him—too much to ruin his life. While they were not hurling the questions that U.S. reporters would have, they asked for her identity.

And once they learned who she was—the widow of a Russian mobster—they would not welcome her as they did their prince. They would believe, as she already did, that she was not good enough for him. His grandfather was right, and certainly Sebastian knew, that royalty needed to marry royalty, not commoners like her.

AFTER A WEEK OF WAITING for the sheriff to close the shootings at the ranch and clear him of any wrongdoing, Sebastian had finally been free to leave Dumont. He could have invoked diplomatic immunity and left earlier, but he had wanted to keep the sheriff as an ally, so that Antoine had someone else watching his back because Sebastian could not.

It had also taken him a week to talk Jessica into

coming with him for her and Samantha's safety. But while she was with him in body, that spirit of hers for which he had fallen so hard was not present.

The Jessica he knew so intimately and loved so deeply really hadn't come to Barajas with him. Now he stood outside the door to her guest suite. She had already tucked Samantha into bed. He'd checked on the little girl himself, kissing her forehead as she snuggled under the blankets. His heart ached from swelling so much with the love that filled it for her.

He would do anything for her. Or for her mother. Even let them go if he had to—if she really wanted to go. He couldn't hold on to her like Evgeny had.

Perhaps Antoine was wrong. Perhaps she did not love him. But he wouldn't know unless he asked. So he lifted his hand and rapped his knuckles against the glossy mahogany panels.

The door opened on silent hinges—the only sound the slight catch of her breath as Jessica stared up at him. She'd washed out the red dye, leaving her hair a warm chocolate brown. And she'd had it cut so that it curled softly around her face, making her look more like a teenager than a thirty-one-year-old single mother.

"You didn't need to check on us," she said. "We're quite comfortable."

"Are *we?*" he asked, because he sure as hell wasn't comfortable, not with her inside his house but still so far out of reach.

"Yes," she said. "Samantha is, too. You already know

that, though, because you just checked on her. I heard you go into her room."

"She was fast asleep." He skimmed his gaze down Jessica's body. She'd wrapped a terry-cloth robe around her sexy curves, cinching it tight around her slim waist. "Why aren't you…if you're so comfortable here?"

"Of course I'm comfortable. It's a palace." She spun in the middle of the floor, her bare feet sliding easily across the marble. "It's literally a palace."

"It sounds like that makes you uncomfortable."

She lifted her slender shoulders in a slight shrug. "Maybe it just makes me feel guilty."

"Guilty?"

Her beautiful face flushed with rosy color. "I shouldn't be here."

"Jessica—"

"I should be back at the ranch," she said. "I should be taking care of Helen. It's my fault she got hurt so badly."

"It's Evgeny's fault," he corrected her. "Not yours. She loves you."

Tears glistening in her eyes, she nodded. "That's why I should be back there, helping her clean up the mess left at the ranch."

"I am making certain that the mess is cleaned up."

She smiled. "You're doing more than cleaning up. You're redoing the whole place."

"You would not accept the reward, so I gave it to a good cause."

"Fulfilling Helen's dream of converting her ranch into a women's shelter from domestic abuse."

"It already was," he said. "She offered you shelter all those years."

"Now you're offering me shelter." She expelled a ragged little sigh. "When all this is over, and I'm sure Samantha is safe, I will stop being a charity case."

"You are not a charity case." Not with her stubborn pride.

She snorted. "Yeah, right. I'm just another responsibility you don't need right now. I know you'd rather be in Dumont, looking for your friend and watching over your brother."

"There is no place I'd rather be," he said and stepped inside her room and closed the door. "And I'm not offering you shelter or charity."

He reached out, pleased when she didn't flinch— when instead her face flushed a deeper rose and her eyes grew dark, her pupils dilating as she stared up at him. Unable to resist her any longer, he lowered his head and covered her mouth with his. He kissed her hungrily, parting her lips to taste her unique sweetness.

She planted her palms against his chest and eased him back. Panting for breath, she asked, "What are you offering me?"

"My heart."

She shook her head, as if trying to shake herself awake. "No."

"You won't take my heart?" He stepped back, reached

into his pocket and pulled out the small velvet box. "You won't take my ring?"

She gasped in surprise.

He popped the box open to the oval diamond solitaire that caught the light of the chandelier hanging over her bed. "You won't take my name?"

"You can't offer any of these things to me," she said with a wistful sigh.

"Why not?" Did she not love him? Had Antoine been wrong? Perhaps there was a first time for everything. But she had risked her life for his.

"You are a prince. You can't marry a woman like me."

"A woman like you?"

"I am not royalty," she said. "But my life is a royal mess. I was married to a Russian mobster. I'm a single mother. I would ruin your public image."

"It does not matter to me if you are not royalty."

"But you dated only princesses." She threw his words back at him.

And for a moment he regretted ever telling her. But then he was glad that he had because they had no secrets from each other. "I was trying to please a man I could never please. Just because I am my father's son, I would never make my grandfather happy. But he was wrong about my father. You were right. He was a brave man who fought to keep his family safe. He failed, but at least he had the guts to try."

She shook her head with regret. "I don't think I have

the guts to try. I'm not the kind of woman who can marry a prince."

"You have no idea what kind of woman you are," he said with a sigh. "I told you before what kind of woman you are. Strong and brave and resilient. And so very smart."

"Smart enough to know that marrying me will hurt you."

"The only thing that will hurt me is if you tell me that you don't love me as much as I love you."

Tears glistened in her eyes and trickled down her cheeks. In the past week the swelling had gone down, and the bruising had faded. "It's because I love you that I can't accept your ring or your name. Marrying me would hurt you. And I would never do anything to hurt you."

"What do you think is going to happen if you accept my proposal? I am not an elected official," he reminded her.

"But can't princes and kings be overthrown?"

"So you think my marrying you will cause a civil uprising?" he asked, unable to stop a laugh from slipping out.

Pride lifted her chin. "Your country won't approve."

"My country trusts my judgment," he said with his own pride. "I thought you trusted me, too."

"I do."

"Then trust that I know what is best for me. You are best for me. You and Samantha are my world," he said, his love overflowing his too-full heart to spill into his voice. "Losing Barajas would not hurt me as much as losing you two."

She blinked back her tears. "You won't lose your country."

He uttered her name as a protest of her refusal. "Jessica—"

She held out her left hand. "And you won't lose me or Samantha. I will accept your love, Sebastian, as long as you accept mine."

That emotion swelling from his heart to his throat made it difficult for him to speak. He had to swallow hard before he could ask, "Jessica Peters, will you do me the honor of becoming my wife?"

"I will be honored to be your wife," she replied.

He slid the ring onto her finger, not surprised that it was a perfect fit. Just like the two of them. He stood up, lifted her in his arms and swung her around as joy exploded inside him.

He had never been so happy….

Jessica smiled at him, like Samantha did—with that light and warmth that reached so deep inside him. Then she reached for him, tugging open his buttons and unzipping his pants. He pushed the robe from her shoulders so that she stood naked before him. That light of happiness and love radiated from her skin so that she glowed like an angel.

"I love you so much." He said the words against her lips, as he took her mouth. Then he laid her on the bed and took her. As he thrust inside her, he ran his lips down her chin and neck to the swell of her full breasts.

She locked her legs around his waist and met his thrusts, skimming her callused fingers up and down his back. She clutched his butt, pulling him deeper inside her.

They came together, screaming each other's name. And when Sebastian pressed his cheek to hers, it wasn't just her tears that dampened his skin.

"It's real," she murmured. "I'm not dreaming."

"No." He lifted her hand so that the diamond reflected the light. "Because we would both have to be dreaming the same dream."

"We are," she said. "And we just made someone else's dream come true."

"SAMANTHA..." JESSICA GENTLY nudged her daughter awake.

The little girl sleepily blinked her pretty eyes open and stared up at her mother. Sebastian sat next to her on the bed, his arm around her shoulders. "What, Mommy? Is it mornin' already?"

"No." Jessica hadn't been able to wait until morning to share their joy. "You can go back to sleep in just a few minutes."

"'Kay..." Samantha rubbed a knuckle in her eye and focused. "Hi, Sebastian..."

"Hi, sweetheart."

"Remember when you asked me if Sebastian was a real prince?" Jessica asked.

Samantha nodded. "Yeah, when we first saw him on TV. And Helen said princes can't be cowboys. But Sebastian is both."

Sebastian chuckled. "Obviously she hasn't seen me ride yet. Uncle Antoine is the cowboy prince. Not me."

"But he is a prince," Jessica said. "And now you and I are going to be princesses."

"Because he kissed you…like Sleeping Beauty," Samantha said, probably remembering the night in his hotel suite. "He kissed you and woke you up."

His protection and his love had awakened Jessica from the nightmare she'd been living. Finally she had found a man she could trust with her heart—her true Prince Charming. "Yes, he woke me up. And he proposed. I'm going to be his wife, honey."

"And you're going to be my daughter," Sebastian said.

"So that'll make me a princess?"

Jessica nodded.

"Will I get to wear a crown like in my fairy tales?"

"This isn't a fairy tale," Jessica said. "It's real." Their love and their family were wonderfully real.

* * * * *

COWBOYS ROYALE continues in July,
with a gripping story by reader favorite
Carla Cassidy. Look for it wherever
Harlequin Intrigue books are sold!

INTRIGUE

COMING NEXT MONTH

Available April 12, 2011

Selene wanted nothing to do with the father of her son, Alex; but Aristedes had other plans...that included them.

Read on for an sneak peek from
THE SARANTOS SECRET BABY by Olivia Gates,
available April 2011, only from Harlequin Desire.

"You were right to turn my marriage offer down," Aristedes said.

And Selene found her voice at last, found the words that would not betray the blow he'd dealt her. "Thanks for letting me know. You didn't have to come all the way here, though. You could have just let it go. I left yesterday with the understanding that this case is closed."

Before the hot needles behind her eyes could dissolve into an unforgivable display of stupidity and weakness, she began to close the door.

The door stopped against an immovable object. His flat palm.

"I can't accept that." His voice was low, leashed.

What did her tormentor mean now? Was he ending one game only to start another?

She raised eyes as bruised as her self-respect to his, found nothing there but solemnity and determination.

Before she could voice her confusion, he elaborated. "I never let anything go unless I'm certain it's unworkable. I realize I made you an unworkable offer, and that's why I'm withdrawing it. I'm here to offer something else. A workability study."

She leaned against the door, thankful for its support and partial shield. "Your son and I are not a business venture you can test for feasibility."

His gaze grew deeper, made her feel as if he was trying to delve into her mind, take control of it. "It's actually the other way around. I'm the one who would be tested."

She shook her head. "Why bother? I know—and *you* know—you're not workable. Not with me."

His spectacular eyebrows lowered over eyes she felt were emitting silver hypnosis. "You're right again. Neither you nor I have any reason to believe that isn't the truth. The only truth. It might be best for both you and Alex to never hear from me again, to forget I exist. But then again, maybe not. I'm only asking for the chance for both of us to find out for certain. You believe I'm unworkable in any personal relationship. I've lived my life based on that belief about myself. I never really had reason to question it. But I have one now. In fact, I have two."

Find out what happens in
THE SARANTOS SECRET BABY by Olivia Gates,
available April 2011, only from Harlequin Desire.

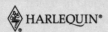

SPECIAL EDITION

Life, Love, Family and Top Authors!

In April, Harlequin Special Edition features
four *USA TODAY* bestselling authors!

FORTUNE'S JUST DESSERTS
by *MARIE FERRARELLA*
Follow the latest drama featuring the ever-powerful
and passionate Fortune family.

YOURS, MINE & OURS
by *JENNIFER GREEN*
Life can't get any more chaotic for Amanda Scott.
Divorced and a single mom, Amanda had given up on
the knight-in-shining-armor fairy tale until a friendship
with Mike becomes something a little more....

THE BRIDE PLAN (*SECOND-CHANCE BRIDAL* MINISERIES)
by *KASEY MICHAELS*
Finding love and second chances for others is
second nature for bridal-shop owner Chessie.
But will *she* finally get her second chance?

THE RANCHER'S DANCE
by *ALLISON LEIGH*
Return to the Double C Ranch this month—where love, loss
and new beginnings set the stage for Allison Leigh's latest title.

*Look for these titles and others in April 2011
from Harlequin Special Edition, wherever books are sold.*

www.eHarlequin.com

SEUSA0411

Harlequin® Blaze™

red-hot reads

Sunny, sensual Hawaiian spring break…again!

Three best girlfriends are recapturing an amazing spring-break vacation they had a decade ago.

First on the beach is former attorney and all-around good girl Mia Butterfield. Meeting up with her boyfriend of old is a bust, so she's shocked when her hero turns out to be someone she'd never have expected…

Find out who it is in

SECOND TIME LUCKY

by acclaimed author

Debbi Rawlins

Available from Harlequin Blaze® April 2011

Part of the sensual miniseries,

Spring Break

Part 2: Delicious Do-Over (May)

Harlequin®

A *Romance* FOR EVERY MOOD™